SILENT GUARDIANS

Silent Guardians

The beginning

Patrick Hilton

Published by Spines
ISBN: 979-8-89383-563-2

For the ones who have fallen and the ones who are still here.

Words can't say enough!

Contents

CHAPTER 1

RETRIBUTION

In the dark streets of the village, a shadow moved with purpose. His footsteps were silent on the pavement. The figure was clad in black. A lethal weapon was strapped to his side. This was no ordinary person; he was a former Marine, now turned vigilante, on a mission of retribution. Mark Stevens moved through the dimly lit alleyways. His senses heightened, and his muscles coiled with tension. The weight of his past. The memories of battles fought, and lives lost, fueled his relentless pursuit of those who preyed on the innocent. Mark Stevens was no stranger to darkness. The shadows seemed to embrace him, cloaking his movements as he glided through the labyrinthine alleyways of the Village. His training as a Marine had honed his senses to a razor's edge, allowing him to navigate the dimly lit streets with silent efficiency. Every step he took was deliberate, every sense on high alert as he scanned his surroundings for any sign of danger. The weight of his past - the missions, the battles, the fallen comrades - bore down on him, a constant reminder of the cost of warfare. It was this burden that now drove him forward, spurring him on in his quest for justice.

Mark's keen eyes scanned the graffiti-covered walls, the flickering streetlights casting long shadows across his path. He knew that within the darkness lurked those who preyed on the innocent, feeding on the vulnerability of the unsuspecting. It was this knowledge that hardened his resolve, steeling his heart against the horrors he had witnessed and the atrocities he had endured.

As he neared his target, a notorious terrorist faction known for their brutal tactics and iron- fisted control of the neighborhood, a quiet fury kindled within Mark. These were the perpetrators of crimes against the helpless, the oppressors who revealed in their power over others. They had underestimated him, thinking he was just another face in the crowd, but they would soon learn that the former Marine had a different set of rules.

With practiced ease, Mark retrieved his weapon, the weight familiar in his hand. It was a tool of retribution, a symbol of the justice he sought to mete out to those who thought themselves untouchable. His grip tightened; his resolve unyielding as he prepared to confront the darkness head-on.

In that moment, as he stood at the threshold of confrontation, Mark Stevens embodied the spirit of retribution. His mission was clear, his purpose was unwavering - to be the avenging angel that struck fear into the hearts of the wicked, to be the beacon of hope for those who had been cast into the shadows. And as he stepped forward, ready to face whatever lay ahead, a righteous fury blazed in his eyes, casting a defiant light in the midst of the darkness that surrounded him. As he navigated the labyrinthine streets, Mark's mind flashed back to the moment that had changed everything. It was a sweltering day in a war-torn village, the air thick with smoke and the stench of death. Mark and his comrades had been on a routine patrol when they stumbled upon a scene of unspeakable horror - an innocent family slaughtered in cold blood, their bodies left to rot in the sun.

The memory of that fateful day still haunted Mark as he traversed the winding alleyways, his mind involuntarily replaying the gruesome images etched into his soul. The village, once teeming with life and laughter, now lay in shambles, a stark reminder of the brutality of war. The sweltering heat beat down on Mark's back, mirroring the intensity of the emotions roiling within him. The acrid smell of smoke and decay lingered in the air, a bitter reminder of the senseless violence he had witnessed. As he and his fellow soldiers had turned the corner that day, their routine patrol had transformed into a nightmare. The sight of the slaughtered family, their bodies scattered like discarded dolls, had seared itself into Mark's consciousness. The lifeless eyes of the children, frozen in expressions of terror and disbelief, haunted his every step. The once vibrant village square now lay desolate and silent, a chilling tableau of the horrors that war could inflict on the innocent.

In that moment, Mark felt a torrent of emotions surge within him - rage, sorrow, guilt. He had sworn an oath to protect the defenseless, yet here he was, standing amidst the aftermath of unspeakable atrocities. The weight of responsibility threatened to crush him, a heavy burden that no amount of training could prepare him for. As he walked through the shadowed alleyways, the memories of that day served as a constant reminder of why he continued to fight.

The faces of the slain family fueled his determination to seek out those responsible, to bring them to justice and ensure that such senseless bloodshed would not go unpunished. Mark's jaw clenched in grim determination as he forged ahead, his path illuminated by the

Aickering streetlights casting long shadows on the cobblestones. The scars of that day ran deep, but they had not dimmed his resolve. With each step he took, he vowed to honor the memory of the fallen family, to be their voice in a world that too often turned a blind eye to the suffering of the innocent. That image had seared itself into Mark's soul, igniting a fire within him that refused to be extinguished. He had sworn to himself then, that he would never again stand idly by in the face of such senseless brutality. And so, he had traded his uniform for shadows, his bullets for justice, becoming a force to be reckoned with in the dark underbelly of the Village.

In the wake of that harrowing experience, Mark had made a solemn vow to himself - a promise forged in the crucible of grief and anger. The image of the slaughtered family lingered in his mind like a scar. A constant reminder of the inhumanity that lurked in the shadows of the world. Determined to make a difference, Mark had decided to shed his uniform and embrace a new identity - one that operated beyond the constraints of law and order. He became a ghost in the village, moving unseen through the labyrinthine streets, his presence felt but never detected.

Gone were the days of following orders and fighting on the front lines; now, Mark's battlefield lay in the hidden recesses of the village, where danger lurked around every corner. He had traded his bullets for a different kind of ammunition - information, leverage, and a relentless commitment to seeking out the truth. With a steely resolve that matched the determination etched on his face, Mark had honed his skills as a master of deception and subterfuge. He navigated the treacherous waters of the criminal underworld with a cunning that belied his military training, earning a reputation as a force to be reckoned with.

No longer bound by the rules of engagement, Mark operated with a single-minded focus on one goal - justice. He sought out those responsible for the atrocities he had witnessed, striking fear into the hearts of the guilty and offering solace to the victims left in their wake. In the shadows of the village, Mark's presence loomed large, a silent avenger for those who had been denied justice. His actions spoke volumes where words fell short, a testament to the unshakeable resolve that burned within him like a flame - a flame that would never be extinguished until he had fulfilled his promise to the innocent souls whose lives had been cut brutally short.

Every gunshot echoed the cries of the fallen, every blow struck was a testament to the lives lost. Mark's inner demons drove him forward, pushing him to root out the evil that festered in the city's veins. With every criminal he brought to justice, he hoped to find a flicker of peace amidst the storm raging inside him. The cacophony of gunfire served as a haunting symphony for each bullet an echo of the cries of the innocent who had fallen to the merciless hands of the wicked. Every strike delivered in the name of justice was a solemn tribute to the lives that had been unjustly cut short. Mark felt the weight of each blow in his bones, a constant reminder of the burden he carried - a burden forged from the anguish and suffering of those who had been wronged. His inner demons, relentless in their torment, drove him ever forward, urging him to confront the darkness that threatened to consume the city.

With unwavering determination, Mark delved deeper into the heart of the criminal underworld, his resolve unshaken by the horrors he uncovered. Each criminal he brought to justice was a small victory in the battle against malevolence, a glimmer of hope in a world plagued by despair. Despite the storm raging within him, Mark pressed on, fueled by the belief that with every act of retribution, he was one step closer to finding peace. His quest for redemption was a tempestuous journey. Fraught with danger and uncertainty, but he remained steadfast in his mission to extinguish the flames of evil that threatened to engulf the Village. Each criminal he brought to justice was a step towards reconciliation, a step towards finding solace amidst the chaos that raged within him.

As he crept closer to his latest target, a notorious warlord known for his ruthlessness and brutality, Mark's heart pounded in his chest. The time for retribution had come. The Marine within him, tempered by fire and forged in the crucible of war, stood ready to mete out justice to those who believed themselves above the law. As Mark closed in on his latest quarry, a sense of urgency pulsed through his veins, his heart echoing the rhythm of his determination.

The darkness of the night enveloped him like a shroud, masking his movements as he approached the lair of the infamous warlord, a figure whose very name struck fear into the hearts of even the bravest souls. Memories of past battles and fierce comrades-in-arms filled Mark's mind, invoking the spirit of the Marine within him that had been honed in the crucible of conflict. The trials of war had not only shaped his body but also hardened his resolve, preparing him for the challenges that lay ahead. With each step closer to his target, Mark's muscles tensed with anticipation, his mind calculating every move with precision. The time for justice had arrived, and he stood poised to confront the ruthless criminal whose tyranny had terrorized the village for far too long.

As he readied himself to face the crime lord, a steely determination settled in Mark's gaze, reflecting the fire that burned within him. In that moment, he embodied the spirit of a warrior, a sentinel of righteousness standing against the forces of darkness. The line between predator and prey blurred as Mark prepared to unleash his own brand of justice upon those who believed themselves untouchable. Mark emerged from the shadows, a silent wraith cutting through the darkness, his resolve unbreakable, his aim true. In that moment, there was no fear, no hesitation - only the unwavering certainty that he was exactly where he was meant to be, exacting a price for the sins of the guilty.

Mark stepped out of the veil of shadows, a figure of righteous retribution moving with purpose and precision. His presence alone cast a palpable sense of unease upon those who dared to witness his silent approach, the air quivering with an invisible tension. With each step, his resolve radiated a fierce determination, a force of nature fueled by an unyielding sense of justice. The darkness seemed to part ways before him, as if acknowledging the power that emanated from within him. No trace of doubt clouded his mind; every movement was deliberate, every action calculated with the precision of a finely tuned instrument. There was a steady calmness in his demeanor, a quiet confidence that spoke volumes of the unwavering conviction that burned within him. Mark's eyes gleamed with a steely resolve, reflecting the unfaltering clarity of his purpose.

As he closed in on his target, the weight of his mission bore down upon him, yet he remained undaunted. The burden of responsibility only served to strengthen his resolve, solidifying his commitment to hold the guilty accountable for their transgressions. In that moment, Mark was a force of nature, a harbinger of justice cutting through the darkness with unwavering determination. The echoes of his presence lingered in the air, a testament to the unwavering spirit of retribution that guided his every move.

Mark Stevens had seen too much during his time in the military. The atrocities committed, the lives lost, the injustices that went unpunished. He had tried to leave it all behind when he returned home, but the memories haunted him, pushing him towards a path of vengeance. Mark bore the weight of his military experience like a burden too heavy to shake off. The ghosts of the past, the haunting memories of atrocities witnessed and the senseless loss of lives, followed him like shadows wherever he went. Each image seared into his mind, each injustice etched into his soul, creating a deep and unhealed wound that refused to scar over.

Despite his best efforts to build a new life upon returning home, the echoes of war and suffering trailed behind him, a relentless whisper that grew louder with each passing day. Mark tried to bury the pain, to numb himself to the horrors he had seen, but the memories clawed their way back to the surface, a constant reminder of the darkness that still lingered within him.

The injustices that went unaddressed, the lives lost in vain, gnawed at his conscience like a festering wound. He had witnessed firsthand the brutality of war, the corruption of power, and the callous disregard for human life. The realization that these sins went unpunished, that the guilty walked free while the innocent suffered, ignited a simmering anger within him.

Unable to ignore the call to action, Mark found himself drawn towards a path of vengeance, his sense of justice skewed by the searing memories of the past. The line between right and wrong was blurred in his quest for retribution, the boundaries of morality bending under the weight of his unresolved trauma. As he navigated this turbulent emotional landscape, Mark teetered on the edge of a precipice, torn between the desire for justice and the fear of losing himself to the darkness that threatened to consume him.

The journey towards redemption seemed fraught with peril, with no clear path in sight, as he grappled with his inner demons and the relentless echoes of a past that refused to be silenced. Targeting the criminal underbelly of the village, Mark hunted down those who thought they were untouchable. Drug dealers, human traffickers, corrupt officials - no one was safe from his brand of justice. With military precision, he planned his strikes, leaving no room for error. Mark's pursuit of justice took on a relentless and calculated form as he delved into the murky depths of the criminal underworld that lurked within the village shadows. No longer content to stand idle by while the guilty escaped accountability, he became a one-man force of retribution, targeting those who believed themselves to be beyond the reach of the law.

With a steely resolve born from his military training, Mark sets his sights on dismantling the criminal organizations that wielded power through fear and corruption. Drug dealers peddling poison to the vulnerable, human traffickers preying on the desperate, and corrupt officials colluding in nefarious schemes - all found themselves in the crosshairs of his unwavering quest for justice. Employing the same precision and discipline that had defined his military service, Mark meticulously planned each strike, leaving nothing to chance. Every move was calculated, every decision informed by a deep-seated determination to root out evil at its source. His methods were methodical, his execution flawless, as he moved through the city's darkest corners like a shadowy avenger, striking fear into the hearts of those who believed themselves untouchable.

As he waged his personal war on crime, Mark's reputation as a formidable force began to spread like wildfire through the criminal underbelly of the village. Whispers of a vigilante enforcer, a lone wolf hunting down the predators that preyed on the innocent, sent tremors through the ranks of those who once operated with impunity. The balance of power shifted, the scales of justice tipping in favor of the oppressed and the forgotten, as Mark's relentless pursuit of retribution put the city's underworld on notice. As Mark closed in on his latest target, a notorious warlord responsible for countless deaths in the village, he knew that this would be his most dangerous mission yet. But he was fueled by a righteous fury, a determination to make things right in a world where evil seemed to reign unchecked.

As Mark embarked on his mission to bring down the notorious warlord terrorizing the village, a sense of impending danger loomed over him like a dark cloud. The stakes were higher than ever, with the criminal mastermind responsible for a trail of devastation and heartache that cut deep into the fabric of the community. Undeterred by the risks, Mark channeled his inner resolve and steeled himself for the daunting task ahead. His unyielding commitment to justice burned brightly within him, driving him to confront the darkness head-on and refuse to be swayed by fear or doubt. Every step closer to his target felt like a silent battle being waged in the shadows, each moment fraught with tension and anticipation. As he ventured deeper into the heart of the warlord's stronghold, surrounded by the echoes of past atrocities, Mark knew that he had to tread carefully yet decisively if he wanted to emerge victorious.

The memory of the innocent lives lost at the hands of the warlord fueled Mark's determination, infusing him with a sense of purpose that transcended his own safety. With unwavering focus and a steely resolve, he meticulously planned his approach, leaving no detail overlooked in his quest to bring the perpetrator to justice. As he prepared to face his most formidable foe yet, Mark stood firm in his belief that no evil could withstand the unwavering light of truth and justice. In the face of overwhelming odds, he remained a beacon of hope for those who had suffered at the hands of the warlord, a lone figure willing to sacrifice everything to ensure that righteousness prevailed in a world teetering on the brink of darkness.

CHAPTER 2

THE HUNT

The warlord was holed up in an abandoned warehouse. Mark was not intimidated. He carefully planned his approach, taking out the guards one by one with deadly precision. Mark knew that the key to success lay in stealth and strategy. As he crept closer to the warehouse under the cover of the night, his senses sharpened, every nerve attuned to the slightest movement or sound. The air was thick with tension as he surveyed the surroundings, plotting his next move with the precision of a seasoned predator. With each guard he silently incapacitated, a surge of adrenaline coursed through Mark's veins, fueling his determination to press on despite the ever-present danger. He moved like a shadow, gliding undetected through the darkness, his focus unwavering as he inched closer to his quarry and the promise of justice that awaited within.

The abandoned warehouse loomed ominously in the distance, its windows shattered and doors hanging askew, a testament to the criminal activities that had once thrived within its walls. As Mark approached, he could sense the ominous presence of the warlord lurking within, a formidable adversary who had evaded capture for far too long. As he finally reached the threshold of the warehouse, a palpable tension filled the air, the anticipation of the imminent showdown crackling like electricity between Mark and his target. With a steady hand and steely resolve, he prepared to confront the warlord and deliver the justice that so many had been denied. In that moment, Mark stood as a solitary figure against a backdrop of darkness, a beacon of right-eousness determined to bring an end to the reign of terror that had plagued the city for far too long. With unwavering resolve and a heart filled with righteous fury, he steeled himself for the final showdown that would determine the fate of all involved.

As he made his way towards the warlord's inner sanctum, the sound of gunfire echoed through the empty halls. The leader emerged, a cruel smile on his face as he raised his weapon. But Mark was faster, his training kicking in as he dodged the bullets and returned fire. Mark's training had honed his reflexes to a razor's edge, giving him the split-second advantage he needed to evade the deadly hail of bullets that rained down on him.

With a grace that belied the chaos surrounding him, he moved with fluid precision, each movement a carefully calculated step towards victory. The warlord is cruel smirk faltered as Mark's counterattack caught him off guard, his shots striking true and forcing the criminal mastermind to take cover. The stalemate was broken, the balance of power shifting in an instant as Mark gained the upper hand in their deadly game of cat and mouse. A deadly dance unfolded as the two adversaries engaged in a fierce battle of wills, their gunfire ringing out like a symphony of violence in the empty warehouse. Mark's resolve never wavered; his determination unwavering as he closed the distance between them with lethal intent.

As the smoke cleared and the echoes of gunfire faded, Mark emerged victorious, his eyes steely with triumph as he stood over the defeated warlord. The cruel smile had vanished from the warlord's face, replaced by a look of fear and realization that his reign of terror had come to an end. With the sound of approaching sirens in the distance, Mark knew that justice had been served. The hunt was over, his mission accomplished. As he gazed down at the fallen warlord, a sense of satisfaction washed over him, knowing that he had brought closure to those who had suffered at the hands of this ruthless criminal. And with that, Mark turned and walked away, his purpose fulfilled, leaving behind a legacy of courage and determination in the face of darkness. A fierce battle ensued; the two adversaries were locked in a deadly dance of violence. But Mark's determination was unwavering, his skills honed through years of training. In the end, it was his unwavering sense of justice that gave him the edge, as he finally overpowered the warlord and brought him to his knees.

The tension in the air was palpable as Mark and the warlord faced off in a fierce battle of wills and firepower. Each shot fired echoed through the room, filling the empty space with the sound of violence and chaos. Mark's years of training had prepared him for this exact moment, his senses sharp and his reflexes lightning fast, as he dodged and weaved through the barrage of bullets. With every move, he closed the distance between himself and his enemy, his unwavering determination driving him forward in the face of danger. As the battle raged on, it became clear that it was not just a test of physical prowess, but a clash of ideologies. The warlord represented everything Mark fought against - corruption, cruelty, and injustice. And with every shot fired, Mark's sense of justice burned brighter, giving him the strength to push through the fatigue and keep pressing forward.

Finally, with a well-timed maneuver, Mark gained the upper hand, swiftly disarming the warlord and bringing him to his knees. The once powerful criminal now looked up at Mark with a mixture of fear and defeat in his eyes, knowing that his reign of terror was finally over. With a cool determination, Mark subdued the warlord and ensured that he would face justice for his crimes. As he stood victorious over his fallen enemy, a sense of closure washed over him, knowing that he had made the world a little safer that day. And as the authorities arrived to take the warlord into custody, Mark knew that his unwavering sense of justice had prevailed, and that he had once again proven that even in the darkest of battles, the light of truth and righteousness would always shine through.

CHAPTER 3

REDEMPTION

As the authorities arrived to arrest the warlord and his accomplices, Mark slipped away into the night. His mission was complete, but the fight was far from over. There were still more criminals out there, still more iniustices to be righted. Mark knew that his work was never truly done, for the fight against crime and corruption was an ongoing battle. As he navigated the dark alleyways and dimly lit streets, a sense of purpose burned within him - a drive to bring about redemption, not only for himself but for the world around him.

His encounter with the warlord reinforced his belief in the power of justice and the importance of standing up for what was right. As he moved stealthily through the shadows, he thought about all those who had been victimized by the criminal underworld - innocent people whose lives had been shattered by greed and violence. With each step he took, Mark vowed to continue his crusade against evil, to seek out those who preyed on the vulnerable and to ensure that they faced the consequences of their actions. His determination was unwavering, his resolve unbreakable as he embarked on his next mission to bring hope and healing to a world plagued by darkness.

As the village slumbered and the streets whispered tales of unrest, Mark emerged as a solitary figure, a beacon of light in the midst of shadows. To him, redemption was not just a concept - it was a calling, a purpose that drove him forward with a relentless passion and a steadfast courage. And as he disappeared into the night, ready to face whatever challenges lay ahead, Mark knew that he carried within him the power to make a difference, to bring about change and to create a better, safer world for all. Redemption was not just a word - it was his mission, his reason for being, and he would not rest until justice prevailed and the forces of darkness were vanquished.

But Mark had found something else as well - a sense of redemption, a purpose beyond revenge. With each bad person he took down, he felt a little piece of his soul healed. He knew that he could never erase the past, but he could make a difference in the present. Mark had embarked on his crusade with a heart heavy with pain and a mind clouded by thoughts of vengeance. The scars of his past weighed heavily on his soul, leading him down a dark and treacherous path. But as he delved deeper into his mission to bring criminals to justice, something unexpected began to emerge within him - a glimmer of hope, a flicker of redemption.

With each nefarious individual he confronted and each corrupt operation he dismantled; Mark felt a shift within himself. The sense of satisfaction that came from standing up against wrongdoing and protecting the innocent brought a newfound sense of purpose and fulfillment. It was as if with every act of justice, a burden was lifted from his shoulders, and a spark of light illuminated the shadows of his past. He realized that while he could never undo the mistakes of his youth, he had the power to shape his future and make a positive impact on the world around him. Each criminal he brought to justice was not just a step towards revenge, but a step towards redemption - not only for his own soul but for the community he sought to protect.

As he fought for what was right and just, Mark found solace in the knowledge that he was making a difference, however small, in the lives of those affected by crime and corruption. His actions were no longer driven solely by a desire for retribution but also by a genuine wish to create a better world, a world where justice prevailed and where redemption was not just a far-off dream but a tangible reality. And so, with each step he took and each victory he achieved, Mark's journey towards redemption continued, guided by a newfound sense of purpose, a steadfast commitment to righteousness, and a heart filled with hope for a brighter tomorrow.

And so, Mark continued his mission, a silent guardian watching over the villages, ready to strike at a moment's notice. He was a force to be reckoned with, a beacon of hope in a world that often seemed engulfed in darkness. Mark's presence in the village became more than just a mere vigilante seeking justice - he had evolved into a symbol of hope and protection for its residents. His unwavering commitment to standing up against crime and injustice had earned him a reputation as a silent guardian, a watchful protector who operated from the shadows, ready to intervene at any moment.

The mere mention of Mark Stevens, struck fear into the hearts of criminals, knowing that their nefarious deeds could be met with swift and decisive action. His very existence served as a deterrent to those who sought to exploit the vulnerable and prey on the innocent. But beyond his formidable reputation and the aura of mystery that surrounded him, Mark embodied something more profound - a beacon of hope shining brightly in a world filled with darkness. In times of uncertainty and despair, his presence reassured the citizens that there was someone watching over them, someone fighting for justice and standing up for what was right. Mark's actions inspired others to take a stand against wrongdoing and empowered the community to come together in the face of adversity. His silent crusade served as a reminder that even in the darkest of times, there were still those willing to fight for a better future, to be a ray of light cutting through the shadows.

As he continued his mission, Mark's reputation grew, and his legend spread throughout the villages, becoming a source of inspiration and courage for all who sought to make a difference. His unwavering dedication to the cause of justice and his selfless devotion to protecting the innocent solidified his place as a true hero - a symbol of hope and resilience in a world that sorely needed it. For those who crossed the line, who thought they could escape justice, there was one simple truth they would come to learn - no one was beyond the reach of Mark Stevens. And as long as evil lurked in the shadows, he would be there, ready to bring retribution to those who deserved it.

The reputation of Mark grew far and wide, instilling fear and respect in those who dared to stray onto the wrong side of the law. His relentless pursuit of justice and unwavering determination to uphold what was right sent a clear message to wrongdoers everywhere - no one was untouchable, no one was beyond his reach. Those who sought to evade the consequences of their actions quickly discovered that Mark Stevens was a force to be reckoned with. He operated with precision and purpose, striking fear into the hearts of even the most hardened criminals. His reputation as a relentless pursuer of justice preceded him, making his very name synonymous with retribution for those who had committed unspeakable acts.

Mark's unwavering vigilance and dedication to his cause was a stark reminder to all that evil had no place to hide, no refuge to seek, if he was on the prowl. His presence was a beacon of hope for the downtrodden and a harbinger of justice for the wicked, a living embodiment of the belief that no one could escape the consequences of their deeds. As long as darkness loomed in the shadows, Mark stood as a shining light of justice, a steadfast guardian ready to mete out retribution to those who deserve it. His commitment to righting wrongs and protecting the innocent served as a guiding principle, a moral compass for a city of villages plagued by crime and corruption.

And so, his legend continued to grow, his name whispered in fear and reverence by those who understood the simple truth - no one was beyond the reach of Mark Stevens.

CHAPTER 4

GROWING UP

Mark Stevens grew up in the outskirts of a bustling city nestled in the picturesque landscape of Northeast Indiana. Surrounded by rolling hills, lush forests, and winding rivers, his childhood was filled with the sights and sounds of nature's beauty. The small-town charm coupled with the proximity to a vibrant urban center provided Mark with a unique blend of rural tranquility and urban excitement.

As a young boy, Mark spent his days exploring the verdant corn fields and creeks that stretched for miles around his home. He developed a deep appreciation for the natural world, finding solace and inspiration in the quietude of the countryside. The fresh air, the rustle of leaves in the wind, and the songs of birds overhead became the backdrop to his formative years. Despite the idyllic setting, Mark was no stranger to hard work and perseverance. Growing up on the outskirts meant a strong sense of community and self-reliance, traits that were instilled in him from a young age. He learned the value of a honest day's labor and the importance of loyalty and integrity, principles that would shape his character for years to come.

As he navigated the transition from boyhood to adolescence, Mark was drawn to the pulsating energy of the nearby city. It's one skyscraper soaring high into the sky, its bustling streets filled with a tapestry of sights and sounds - it captivated him with its promise of endless possibilities and opportunities. The city's eclectic cultural scene, diverse population, and dynamic pace fueled his curiosity and ignited his ambition.

Mark's upbringing on the outskirts of Northeast Indiana provided him with the perfect blend of tranquility and excitement, laying the foundation for the man he would become. The balance of rural simplicity and urban vibrancy shaped his perspective, instilling in him a deep appreciation for nature's beauty and a drive to reach for new horizons. Mark Stevens hailed from a proud lineage with a history deeply intertwined with military service. The tradition of serving his country ran through his family tree, tracing all the way back to the tumultuous period of the China Boxer Rebellion. His ancestors had heeded the call to duty, bravely venturing into the unknown and facing the challenges of a distant land in the service of a greater cause.

Growing up, Mark was regaled with tales of valor and sacrifice passed down through the generations. Stories of resilience in the face of adversity, camaraderie on the battlefield, and unwavering dedication to duty painted a vivid picture of his family's legacy of military service. These narratives instilled in him a deep respect for the sacrifices made by his forebears and fueled his own sense of duty and honor. His father, a stoic and disciplined man who had served his country with unwavering loyalty, guided Mark with a firm yet nurturing hand. The lessons learned from his father's experiences in the military were not just anecdotes from a bygone era; they were living, breathing examples of courage, discipline, and selflessness that shaped Mark's own values and aspirations.

As a young man, Mark felt the tug of his family's military heritage, knowing that the path of service and sacrifice was not just a tradition to uphold but a calling to fulfill. The stories of his ancestors and the values instilled by his father imbued him with a sense of purpose and a desire to make a meaningful contribution to his country and the world. Through the generations, the legacy of military service in Mark's family had been a source of pride and inspiration, a thread that connected him to the past and guided him towards the future. The echoes of bravery and selflessness reverberated in his heart, propelling him forward on a path of honor and duty, in homage to those who had come before him.

Mark Stevens had always walked a solitary path, finding solace in his own company and comfort in the quiet moments of solitude. From a young age, he had been content to retreat into his thoughts, pursuing his interests and passions with a fierce independence that set him apart from his peers. While others sought out companionship and social connections, Mark found his own inner world to be a sanctuary, a place where he could explore his thoughts and emotions without distractions. His tendency towards solitude did not stem from a lack of social skills or a disdain for others; rather, it was a conscious choice he made to prioritize introspection and self-discovery. He relished the freedom of being alone, finding peace and tranquility in the absence of external noise and infuences. In solitude, he could fully immerse himself in his thoughts, exploring ideas and emotions with a depth and intensity that was unmatched in the company of others.

Over the years, Mark's solitary nature had become a defining trait, shaping his interactions with the world and influencing the choices he made. While some may have perceived him as aloof or distant, those who knew him well understood that his preference for solitude was not a barrier but a bridge to deeper conversations and connections. In his solitude, he cultivated a rich inner life, filled with introspection, creativity, and a unique perspective on the world around him. Despite his solitary nature, Mark had developed strong bonds with a select few individuals who shared his values and understood his need for solitude. These rare connections served as anchors in a world that often seemed overwhelming and chaotic, providing him with the support and companionship he needed without sacrificing his independence or inner peace.

As he walked his solitary path through life, Mark found moments of beauty and meaning in the quiet spaces between the noise and bustle of the world. His solitude was not a burden to bear but a gift to cherish, a source of strength and inspiration that fueled his creative spirit and nurtured his soul. In his solitude, he discovered a profound sense of self-awareness and authenticity, embracing his uniqueness and individuality with a quiet confidence that radiated from within.

CHAPTER 5

BACK TO BUSINESS

Mark Stevens had been diligently working in the construction industry, digging ditches for a cable construction company, a job that demanded physical strength and resilience. Despite the grueling nature of the work, he approached each day with determination and a strong work ethic, knowing that every task completed brought him one step closer to his goals.

As he toiled under the sun, sweat soaking his brow and hands calloused from the hard labor, Mark found a sense of purpose and satisfaction in his work. His time in the military had instilled in him a deep sense of discipline and dedication, qualities that he carried with him into his civilian life. Digging ditches was not glamorous work, but it was honest and noble, a way for him to make a living and provide for himself with grit and perseverance.

One day, while he was in the midst of his work, a sleek black sedan pulled up to the construction site, catching his attention. As he wiped the sweat from his brow, he recognized the face that emerged from the driver's seat, a familiar figure from his past. The sudden appearance of this individual sparked a flurry of memories and emotions within Mark, stirring up a mixture of curiosity and apprehension. The figure approached him with a confident stride. Their expression unreadable, as they stood before each other. Mark's mind raced with questions and possibilities, trying to decipher the intent behind this unexpected visit. Was it a chance encounter, or was there a specific reason for their presence at his workplace? Whatever the case may be, Mark braced himself for the conversation that was about to unfold, ready to face whatever challenges or opportunities lay ahead.

As the two engaged in conversation, old wounds were reopened and buried grievances resurfaced. The encounter presented Mark with a choice - to confront the past and seek closure, or to let bygones be bygones and move forward with his life. In that moment, he realized that this unexpected reunion held the potential to alter the course of his future, leading him down a path he had never anticipated. Despite the uncertainty and unease that lingered in the air, Mark knew that he was ready to face whatever challenges awaited him. The encounter with the familiar face from his past served as a reminder of how interconnected our lives can be, weaving together the threads of fate and destiny in ways we may never fully understand. With a steady resolve and a determined spirit, Mark stood ready to embrace the unknown and carve out a new chapter in his life's journey.

"Mr. Green", we will call him, let out a hearty laugh, his voice cutting through the dusty air of the construction site. With a bemused expression on his face, he jokingly questioned, 'What the hell are you doing this for?' His words were met with a chuckle from his fellow workers, who paused in their tasks to witness the light-hearted exchange. I straightened up, wiping my hands on my jeans as I turned to face Mr. Green. The nickname was fitting, given his surname's reference to the vibrant color that contrasted sharply with the earthy tones of our work environment. Despite his jovial demeanor, there was an air of authority about him that commanded respect among the crew.

Before I could respond, Mr. Green's expression shifted, and he relayed a message that caught me off guard. "The boss sent me' he continued, his tone more solemn now. 'Mr. White wants you to go see him. The mention of Mr. White, our enigmatic leader whose presence loomed large over the company, instantly piqued my curiosity and set my pulse racing. Questions swirled in my mind as I tried to make sense of the unexpected summons. What could Mr. White possibly want to see me about? How had I managed to attract his attention among the sea of Black Op Contractors listed on his payroll? With a mix of trepidation and anticipation, I locked eyes with Mr. Green, silently urging him to provide more details.

Sensing my eagerness, Mr. Green cut to the chase. How long before you're up and running he inquired, his gaze probing. Without hesitation, I made a split-second decision. I dropped the shovel I had been holding, the clang of metal hitting the ground echoing in the space between us, and declared. 'Now'! The determination in my voice surprised even me. In that moment, I felt a surge of adrenaline coursing through my veins, propelling me forward with a new found sense of purpose. Whatever awaited me in the presence of Mr. White, I was ready to face it head-on, confident in my abilities and resolved to make the most of this unexpected opportunity.

As I followed Mr. Green towards the waiting sedan, the anticipation of what lay ahead mingled with the uncertainty of the unknown. Little did I know that this fateful encounter would mark the beginning of a new chapter in my life, one that would test my limits, push me out of my comfort zone, and ultimately lead me down a path of transformation and self-discovery.

After arriving at the airport, I made my way to hangar number 9. A nondescript building tucked away from the bustling terminals. The scent of jet fuel lingered in the air, mixing with the sounds of engines humming in the distance. As I entered the dimly lit space, a sense of solemnity washed over me, knowing that this was where I would make my final preparations. With a steely resolve, I began the process of cleaning up, methodically disposing of all personal items that linked me to my past life. Each memento held a memory, a piece of the person I was leaving behind. I moved with a sense of detachment, pushing down any emotions that threatened to surface as I shed my old identity to embrace a new, unknown future.

As the weight of my actions settled on my shoulders, I reached for pen and paper to compose my final words. The act of writing my death letter felt surreal, the words flowed from pen to paper with a sense of finality. I poured out my thoughts, my regrets, and my hopes onto the page, knowing that this would be the last communication I would ever send to those I left behind. Once the letter was complete, I sealed it in a plain envelope. The gravity of the situation hitting me like a ton of bricks. With a trembling hand, I placed the envelope in the designated box, following the standard procedures that marked this somber ritual. The clang of the lid closing echoed in the empty hangar, a stark reminder of the irreversible decision I had made.

Taking a moment to collect myself, I stood in the quiet solitude of hangar number 9, feeling the weight of my choices pressing down on me. The uncertainty of what lay ahead loomed large, but deep within me, a flicker of determination burned bright. Ready to embark on this final journey, I steeled myself for what was to come, knowing that this was a turning point, a moment that would define the course of my destiny. The rush of adrenaline as the wind whips past me, the exhilaration of freefalling through the sky - these are the moments that captivate me.

I have always had a fascination with planes, but it's not the act of flying that truly ignites my passion. It's the heart-pounding thrill of jumping out of them, leaping into the great unknown with nothing but the open air below me. There is a certain freedom in skydiving, a feeling of weightlessness and liberation that cannot be replicated on solid ground. As I soar through the clouds, the world shrinks below me, and for a fleeting moment, all my worries and fears are left behind. It's a sensation like no other, a pure, unadulterated joy that pulses through my veins with each jump.

But when it comes to flying big birds into hot zones, my feelings shift. The thought of being loaded for World War III, hurtling towards danger and uncertainty, leaves me uneasy. The tension in the air, the weight of the mission pressing down on my shoulders - it's a stark contrast to the pure thrill of skydiving. The stakes are higher, the risks more pronounced, and the consequences far more grave. While I may revel in the rush of jumping out of planes, the prospect of being part of a high-stakes operation in a war zone fills me with a sense of unease. I prefer the freedom of the skies, the rush of adrenaline as I hurtle towards the earth, over the weight of conflict and the burden of war. In the quiet solitude of my freefall, I find a sense of peace that eludes me in the chaos of battle.

As hunger gnaws at my stomach and the absence of any sign of cart service looms large, I can't help but feel a sense of unease creeping in. The Serbian pilot, with a penchant for vodka that seems boundless, sits in the cockpit with a carefree demeanor that borders on reckless. He raises his glass with a confident smirk, downing the fiery liquid as if it were the elixir of life itself. In the cramped confines of the cockpit, the smell of alcohol mingles with the mechanical hum of the plane, creating a heady atmosphere that is equal parts intoxicating and unnerving. The pilot's casual attitude towards his drink of choice is both intriguing and disconcerting, as he jokes about it being his "spirit drink" with a twinkle in his eye. As we soar through the turbulent skies, I can't help but wonder if the pilot's jovial spirit will be enough to guide us safely to our destination. Will his unwavering confidence in the face of uncertainty be our salvation or our downfall? I can only hope that his skill and experience outweigh his love for vodka, and that our journey will end not in tragedy, but in triumph.

With each passing moment, the rumble of the plane and the clink of the pilot's glass creates a strange symphony that underscores the gravity of our situation. In this airborne arena of uncertainty, I cling to the hope that the Russian pilot's spirit can indeed Ay - not just for his own sake, but for all ofus onboard who are depending on him to navigate us through the stormy skies ahead. As the protagonist, Mark Stevens, awakens to the cacophony of rock music and the unexpected air filtering through bullet holes, he finds himself thrust into a perilous situation.

Confusion and disorientation grip him as he tries to make sense of his surroundings. Struggling to gather his bearings, he realizes that he is in an unfamiliar and potentially dangerous location. The sudden appearance of the enigmatic Serbian figure, screaming out urgent commands, sending a shiver down Mark's spine. The urgency in the man's voice hints at imminent danger, propelling Mark into action despite his weariness and hunger. With adrenaline coursing through his veins, Mark knows he must follow the Serbian's instructions if he has any hope of surviving the ordeal. As Mark tentatively edges toward the source of the commotion, he notices the chaos and destruction that surround him. The sight of shattered glass and bullet-riddled walls only amplified his unease. Each step he takes brings him closer to the heart of the unfolding drama, where the Russian stands as a foreboding figure, orchestrating the chaos with an air of authority.

With each passing moment, the stakes grow higher, and Mark realizes that he is entangled in a web of danger from which there may be no easy escape. The Serbian's cryptic last orders hang in the air, their meaning obscured yet laden with a sense of finality. Despite his fear and uncertainty, Mark knows that he must steel himself for whatever lies ahead as he braces for the unknown journey that awaits him. Mark Stevens had encountered his fair share of challenges and dangers in his line of work. However, nothing could have prepared him for the heart-stopping moment when he heard the words he dreaded the most from the Serbian pilot he was flying with.

As the plane soared through the sky, Mark could sense something was amiss. The pilot, seemingly unfazed by the situation, was casually sipping on vodka, and Mark couldn't help but feel a sense of unease creeping over him. Suddenly, the pilot's calm demeanor was shattered by two words that sent chills down Mark's spine. "Oh shit," the pilot muttered, his words laced with a mix of disbelief and panic. Mark's heart skipped a beat as he realized the gravity of the situation. The prospect of "losing another one" flashed through his mind, sending a wave of adrenaline coursing through his veins. In that moment of uncertainty and chaos, Mark's training kicked in, and he sprang into action, assisting the pilot in managing the crisis and ensuring the safety of the aircraft. The harrowing experience tested his limits and pushed him to the edge, but he remained resolute and focused on overcoming the challenges that lay ahead.

Despite the perilous circumstances, Mark's quick thinking and resourcefulness helped avert a potential disaster, demonstrating his resilience and unwavering commitment to his mission. The turbulent flight served as a stark reminder of the dangers inherent in his line of work and reinforced his determination to navigate through any situation with courage and grace. The nightmare scenario unfolded in a split second as Mark found the big plane hurtling towards the ground, his heart pounding in his chest. The deafening sound of impact reverberated through the cabin as the right wing of the aircraft was struck, sending debris flying in all directions. The sight of half the wing disappearing into the darkness outside the window was a chilling realization of the gravity of their predicament. The plane lurched violently to the side, sliding in a chaotic, sideways motion as sparks few, illuminating the night sky in a shower of fiery brilliance.

Contrary to the terrifying situation unfolding around them, the Serbian pilot's laughter filled the air, a stark contrast to the imminent danger they faced. Despite the chaos and uncertainty, the pilot's seemingly carefree demeanor sent shivers down Mark's spine, adding to the surreal nature of their predicament. As the plane skidded to a jarring halt, screeching and groaning in protest to the unforgiving ground, all Mark could think about was escape. The knowledge that there were explosives on board, a ticking time bomb that could detonate with the slightest spark, fueled his sense of urgency and dread. His mind raced with the desperate plea, "Let's get out," echoing like a mantra of survival in the face of impending catastrophe. The realization of the catastrophic consequences that awaited them if the plane erupted into a fiery inferno fueled Mark's determination to find a way out of the dire situation.

With each passing moment, the tension in the cabin mounted, a palpable sense of impending doom hanging heavy in the air. Mark knew that time was working against them, and every second counted in their fight for survival amidst the chaos and destruction surrounding them. As the team hastily disembarked from the damaged airplane, a sense of urgency hung heavy in the air, fueled by the distant echoes of gunfire now fading into the night. The unmistakable sound of AK47s and heavy machine guns had provided a tumultuous backdrop to their harrowing escape, punctuated by sporadic potshots from unseen adversaries.

In the midst of the chaos, Mr. White, the elusive boss man, made his grand entrance as seven trucks rolled onto the scene. With an air of authority and efficiency, the team quickly sprang into action, unloading the valuable cargo from the airplane and transferring it onto the waiting vehicles with practiced precision. As the last of the supplies were loaded onto the trucks, a palpable tension filled the air, with every member of the team acutely aware of the imminent danger lurking in the shadows. In a strategic move to counter the oncoming fighters and regain the upper hand, they swiftly vanished from the landing zone, leaving behind carefully concealed booby traps to disrupt and deter any pursuers.

With the runway cleared and the traps set, a tense silence settled over the abandoned airstrip, broken only by the distant sounds of approaching footsteps and murmurs of the enemy forces. And then, in an explosive crescendo of chaos and destruction, the meticulously laid traps detonated with a deafening boom. In a blinding flash, the unsuspecting fighters fell victim to the sudden onslaught, caught off guard by the cunning tactics of their adversaries. The once-visible airplane vanished into a billowing cloud of smoke and debris, a stark reminder of the high stakes and deadly risks that defined their precarious world of shadows and subterfuge.

As the sun began its ascent in the cloudless sky, casting a scorching heat that swept through the walls of the safe house, the team prepared for their high-stakes mission: a snatch and grab operation that would test their wits and resolve. Under the watchful eye of Mr. White, the enigmatic leader who operated in the shadows of the underworld, the team readied themselves for the task ahead. With provisions of food, ammunition, and supplies meticulously stocked in the safe house, they knew they were well-equipped for the challenges that lay ahead.

Amidst the tense anticipation of the impending operation, a moment of respite presented itself. Finding a quiet corner on the cool floor of the safe house, exhaustion weighed heavily on their weary bodies. As their minds raced with thoughts of the mission ahead, the weariness of constant vigilance and adrenaline-fueled anticipation finally caught up with them, lulling them into a brief, restless sleep.

CHAPTER 6

GO TIME

The dreams that fickered through their minds were fragmented and Aeeting, a hazy mix of past missions, comrades lost in the line of duty, and the ever-looming specter of danger that defined their perilous existence. Yet, despite the turmoil of their subconscious, the fatigue of their bodies ultimately claimed victory, pulling them into a deep, dreamless slumber. In the tranquility of sleep, time seemed to blur, the chaotic reality of their world momentarily suspended as they sought solace in the embrace of rest. And as the sun continued its relentless climb, baking the world outside in searing heat, the occupants of the safe house remained still, locked in a transient state of reprieve before the impending storm of action and uncertainty.

As the clock struck O dark thirty, the darkness of the

early hour enveloped the world outside, a time when most were still lost in the embrace of sleep. But for those who lived in the shadows, for whom missions in the dead of night were a way of life, it was a signal that "go time", had arrived.

Before any operation, no matter how urgent or clandestine, there was a ritual that brought a sense of normalcy to the chaos of their existence. Simple acts that speak volumes about the harsh reality of their chosen path. For this operative, it was the act of eating before a mission, a habit born out of necessity rather than choice. In a world where uncertainty reigned supreme and the next meal was never guaranteed. Finding solace in the simple act of nourishment became a way to ground themselves amidst the turmoil.

With their stomachs full, although temporarily, attention turned to the meticulous preparations that could spell the difference between success and failure in the unforgiving world they inhabited. A thorough weapons check ensured that every firearm was loaded and ready, every blade honed to a deadly edge. Gear check followed suit, with each piece of equipment inspected and secured, ensuring that nothing was left to chance.

But amidst the flurry of activity, there was always one detail that seems to slip through the cracks for some

- gas for the vehicles. The high-stakes world of covert operations, where every second counts, and the margin for error was razor-thin, overlooking something as seemingly mundane as fuel for the getaway vehicles could spell disaster. Recognizing the gravity of such oversights, our operatives made it a point to include a reminder on their mental checklist - a note to self that served as a stark reminder of the unforgiving nature of their world. In the cloak of darkness, with the weight of their mission pressing down upon them, they ensured that every detail was accounted for, leaving nothing to chance as they braced themselves for the unpredictable journey that lay ahead.

The team, a mix of experienced veterans and fresh recruits, was a diverse group with a shared mission ahead. Three of them had already worked together on numerous missions, their bond forged in the crucible of previous operations, while the other two were NFG's, eager to prove themselves in the field. As they gathered for the briefing, Mr. White, the seasoned leader of the team, reiterated the standard operating procedure for the night. With a simple nod, the team acknowledged their familiarity with the protocols - they were all seasoned door kickers, well-versed in the art of breaching and securing targets with precision and efficiency.

Their target for the night was no ordinary mark; he was the money man, a key player with connections to various factions and invaluable intel. While he may not be a high-level target in terms of physical threat, his importance liess in his access and influence within the underground network. The team anticipated encountering a formidable security detail of three to five guards protecting the money man, a challenge they were well-preparedd to face.

As they approached their target location, the team made the strategic decision to ditch their trucks a mile out and proceed on foot, opting for stealth over speed. The cover of night and the element of surprise were on their side, allowing them to approach undetected and avoid unnecessary confrontation. When they reached the money man's residence, they found him still awake, his guards stationed casually at the front door, seemingly oblivious to the imminent threat. The relaxed demeanor of the guards betrayed their unawareness of the danger lurking in the shadows a perfect opportunity for the team to make their move. With bated breath and heightened senses, the team entered a state of readiness. Poised to strike the moment the lights went out, knowing that success hinged on split-second timing and Aawless execution.

As the tension mounted and the stakes rose, the

team braced themselves for the task ahead, knowing that the success of their mission rested on their ability to maintain focus and composure in the face of uncertainty. The distant sound of barking dogs added an extra layer of tension to the already charged atmosphere, heightening the need for sharp situational awareness. Every sound, every movement, could be a potential threat or opportunity, and the team remained vigilant, attuned to the slightest shifts in their surroundings. Amidst the quiet anticipation, a series of events unfolded - two men arrived, one departed, and a pair of cars passed by, each possessing its own unique characteristics. A blue Mercedes and an unfamiliar small vehicle added to the eclectic mix of elements in play, prompting the team to stay alert and observant, ready to adapt to any unforeseen developments that might arise.

The nights cape became a stage for a delicate dance of patience and readiness, as the team maintained their vigil, waiting for the opportune moment to make their move. With nerves of steel and minds sharpened by training and experience, they knew that success hinged on their ability to stay attuned to the ever-shifting dynamics of the situation. Each passing moment brought them closer to the critical juncture when they would need to act decisively, their actions guided by a blend of intuition, strategy, and tactical precision.

As the hours ticked by, the stillness of the night was occasionally punctuated by the loud rumbling snores of the money man, reverberating through the darkness like a freight train cutting through the night. Despite the distraction, the team remained focused on the task at hand. Their readiness and awareness honed to a razor's edge. At last, the moment they had been waiting for arrived - 2.5 hours after lights out, the prearranged signals were discreetly exchanged, setting in motion the carefully orchestrated plan. Each member of the team knew their role and responsibilities, ready to execute their tasks with precision and efficiency.

As they moved into position, the team synchronized their movements seamlessly. Overwatch is in position, while four members stacked up in preparation for whatever lay ahead. The tension in the air was palpable, each member acutely aware of the importance of maintaining stealth and coordination as they advanced towards their objective. Outside, the guards that had been posted as a potential obstacle seemed to have disappeared, leaving a gap in the security that the team would need to exploit. Whether they were simply away on patrol or lulled into a false sense of security by the cover of night remained to be seen, but the team was prepared to handle any situation that arose as they approached their target.

As they closed in on their objective, the team's

resolve was unwavering, their focus unwavering as they braced themselves for the critical moments that lay ahead. With nerves of steel and a shared sense of purpose driving them forward, they were ready to face whatever challenges the night had in store, their actions guided by a combination of strategy, skill, and unwavering determination. After successfully entering the two-story building by bypassing the locked front door, the team found themselves faced with a branching path once inside. To the left, a door stood locked and mysterious, hinting at potential obstacles or hidden secrets beyond. To the right, the inviting glow of a kitchen promised both sustenance and potential clues.

Methodically proceeding, the team carefully assessed the locked door to the left, recognizing the need to navigate its potential challenges. With skilled precision, the door was jimmied open, revealing a room filled with unknown possibilities. Despite the initial caution, thorough inspection revealed no traps awaiting the unwary, allowing the team to proceed unimpeded into the next phase of their mission. Simultaneously, decision-making was swift as one member ascended the staircase, creeping upwards with silent yet purposeful steps. Progressing to the midway point, danger reared its head in the form of trip wire cunningly concealed along the staircase, likely meant to ensnare unwelcome intruders. Swift thinking and steady hands enabled the team member disarmed the trap without a hitch, preserving the mission's momentum without drawing unwanted attention.

As the team advanced cautiously, the distant yet unmistakable sound of snoring persisted, a comforting affirmation that their target remained unaware of their presence. Reaching the bedroom door where the source of the loud snores emanated, a sense of anticipation and readiness filled the air. With bated breath, the team prepared to confront whatever obstacles or surprises lay beyond the threshold, driven by a shared determination to complete their mission successfully.

Following the successful navigation of obstacles within the two-story building, the team encountered an unexpected twist as they cautiously opened the bedroom door. With precision and finesse, the lock was skillfully manipulated as the door creaked open with the utmost care to avoid alerting the occupants of the room. To their surprise, the doorway revealed not just their target, but an entire family huddled together in the same space. In a quick and coordinated manner, the team signaled their next steps to each other, ensuring that every member was ready to act swiftly and decisively. Despite the man in question continuing to snore loudly, the family around him appeared accustomed to the sound, a peculiar yet fortunate circumstance that worked in the team's favor.

Taking swift action to pacify the sleeping individuals without raising alarm, each family member was discreetly subdued, ensuring they would remain unconscious for a substantial duration. With the room now cleared of any potential disruptions, the team swiftly transitioned into extraction mode, beginning with the task of carrying the incapacitated money man out in a coordinated effort. Recognizing the importance of working efficiently and without delay, the team improvised by using a goat cart to transport the heavy-bodied target out of the building and towards their awaiting escape vehicle.

As the team made their way back to the safehouse, Mr. White's location, a surprising development unfolded in the form of an explosion at the local runway. The unexpected turn of events added another layer of urgency and complexity to the mission, emphasizing the need for caution and vigilance throughout their journey. Despite the challenges they faced, the team remained steadfast in their resolve, determined to navigate the changing circumstances and ensure the safety of their mission's target.

The mission took an unexpected turn as the target proved to be unwilling to cooperate through conventional means. Faced with the challenging task of extracting vital information from a reluctant source, the team resorted to flipping him - a strategy that involved applying intense psychological pressure to compel the target to divulge crucial details. Under mounting pressure, the target eventually relented, revealing a wealth of information on video. As the recording captured his confession, he bared his soul, disclosing intricate details about his involvement in various illicit activities. Despite his evident discomfort with the situation, the target expressed that he felt trapped and devoid of alternatives, highlighting the desperation that had led him down a path he now regretted.

For the team tasked with gathering intelligence, their role remained clear: to collect information without passing judgment. In the realm of espionage, objectivity was paramount, and the team understood that their duty was to extract and relay information to the appropriate channels for further analysis. As they prepared to transmit the obtained data to their superiors, the team reflected on the complex nature of their work. While money was often cited as a driving force behind illicit activities, it was clear that behind every operation lay a web of intricate motivations and circumstances. In this instance, the target's choices had been shaped by a harrowing lack of alternatives, illustrating the harsh realities that fueled the underbelly of espionage and clandestine operations.

As the team braced themselves for the next phase of their mission, they remained keenly aware of the weight of the information they carried and the implications it held for their ongoing operations. In a realm where morality is often blurred with necessity, their commitment to extracting the truth, no matter the cost, remained unwavering. As the team's operation at the current site concluded, they swiftly enacted their standard protocol to erase any traces of their presence. The local operative would meticulously clear the house of all incriminating evidence before setting it ablaze, ensuring that no connection could be drawn back to their clandestine activities. This practice of using each safe house only once was a crucial security measure to evade detection and maintain operational secrecy.

With the immediate task completed, the team geared up for their next move, a long journey across the border to rendezvous with an individual who bore the guise of official authority in a foreign land. This meeting with the enigmatic figure named Mr. White held significant importance, as he was set to provide essential information or directives crucial to the team's mission objectives. As the team arrived at the designated meeting point after an arduous 8 hours of driving, Mr. White engaged in a conversation with the "Man in a suit", you know the type, always looking out of place! They spoke for approximately 20 minutes. The nature of their discussion remained shrouded in mystery, with the other team members instructed to remain vigilant and on standby in their vehicle, ready to respond to any unforeseen developments.

The choice to keep one team member, presumably on the lookout or a key operative, stationed in the truck always underscored the need for caution and readiness. In the shadowy world of covert operations, every interaction and exchange of information carry inherent risks, necessitating a constant state of vigilance to mitigate potential threats or dangers.

As the meeting with Mr. White concluded and the team prepared to depart, the air was thick with anticipation and uncertainty. The enigmatic encounter had raised more questions than answers, leaving the team to decipher the implications of their interaction with someone whose presence in their operation seemed incongruous yet indispensable. As they departed the rendezvous point and headed towards their next assignment, the team remained poised for any challenges that lay ahead, knowing that in the world of clandestine operations, trust was a scarce commodity, and every decision held the potential to tip the balance between success and catastrophe.

After the team's rendezvous with Mr. White, they embarked on a tense and silent hour-long journey towards the tarmac where their next mode of transportation awaited them. The sight of another sizable aircraft, its engines humming with anticipation, signaled the next phase of their mission.

CHAPTER 7

JOB WELL DONE

As they approached the waiting plane, the team could sense the adrenaline coursing through their veins, knowing that each mission brought its own unique set of challenges and dangers. The presence of an empty vodka bottle thrown out of the pilot's window hinted at the cavalier attitude of the flight crew, adding an element of unpredictability to the already precarious situation. Despite the surroundings bustling with activity, palpable tension hung in the air as the team prepared to board the aircraft. Each member understood the gravity of the task ahead and the need for precise execution to navigate the intricate web of alliances and betrayals that defined their shadowy world.

As they stepped onto the plane and settled into their seats, a sense of deja vu swept over them. The familiar feeling of anticipation mingled with apprehension, fueling their resolve to see the mission through to its conclusion, no matter the obstacles that lay ahead. With the engines roaring to life and the aircraft hurtling down the runway, the team braced themselves for whatever challenges awaited them at their destination. The rhythmic hum of the plane's engines provided a backdrop to their thoughts, a constant reminder of the dangers and uncertainties that lay beyond the clouds.

As the plane ascended into the night sky, carrying the team towards their next mission, their minds were focused on the task at hand. Each member knew that success was not guaranteed, but their training, skills, and unwavering determination would guide them through the shadows to emerge victorious once more. Here they go again, into the unknown, navigating treacherous waters with steely resolve and unwavering commitment to their mission. The team's unexpected destination of Dubai for a three-day wait left them feeling restless and wary of the potential pitfalls that could accompany such idle time. The mention of money, booze, and the allure of female companionship hinted at the temptations that lay in waiting for the team, threatening to derail their focus and discipline. Our Mission: Sit and wait!

As they settled into their temporary lodgings, the atmosphere was charged with a sense of anticipation mixed with caution. Mark contemplated the challenge of keeping his team in line, knowing that their mission could be compromised by the distractions that beckoned in the vibrant city of Dubai. The Serbian member of the team, known for his boisterous demeanor and penchant for revelry, was already immersed in the excitement of the unexpected layover. His spirited outbursts on the plane, coupled with the mischievous glint in his eye, signaled his readiness to embrace the indulgences that Dubai had to offer.

Mark Stevens couldn't help but chuckle at the Serbian's antics, recognizing the challenge of keeping his comrades in check while also acknowledging the need to maintain their cover and focus on the mission at hand. The nod of approval from the Serbian, seemingly acknowledging their shared victory in navigating the current situation, was met with a sense of camaraderie and mutual understanding. As the team braced themselves for the days ahead in Dubai, Mark knew that he would need to deploy all his diplomatic skills and cunning to ensure that his team emerged unscathed from the glittering city's allure. The prospect of needing an extra week to sober up his comrades only added to the leader's sense of responsibility and determination to keep their mission on track.

With a mix of apprehension and resolve, the team

prepared to weather the storm of temptations that awaited them in Dubai. Each member understood the delicate balance between blending in with the locals and staying true to their mission objectives, a task made all the more challenging by the tantalizing distractions of the city's nightlife and entertainment. As they ventured forth into the bustling streets of Dubai, the team remained vigilant, knowing that their success depended on their ability to navigate the murky waters of deception and seduction. Despite the allure of the city's offerings, the team was united in their determination to see the mission through to its conclusion, no matter the obstacles that lay in their path.

The team's arrival in Dubai brought with it a mix of excitement and trepidation, as they prepared to immerse themselves in the sights and sounds of the vibrant city. While many people may often associate travel with sights to see and places to explore, Mark found himself focused on a more basic yet essential aspect of their journey food. Having a penchant for a good home-cooked meal, Mark couldn't help, but long for the familiar tastes and comforts of a well-prepared dish. Despite the allure of exotic cuisine and fine dining in Dubai, the simple pleasures of a homemade meal held a special place in his heart.

Upon landing in Dubai's airport, the team wasted no

time in executing their standard operating procedure, slipping discreetly through a side entrance to avoid attracting unwanted attention. Stepping out into the bustling city, they were greeted by a cacophony of sounds, the tantalizing smells of street food wafting through the air. Their Serbian pilot, known for his outgoing personality and extensive network of contacts, wasted no time in extending an invitation to show the team around all the hot spots in Dubai. With a mischievous twinkle in his eye, he assured them that he knew everyone worth knowing in the city and promised them an unforgettable experience.

Despite the temptation to join in the Serbian pilot's escapades and explore the city's nightlife and entertainment scene, I declined the offer, mindful of the importance of staying focused on their mission objectives. Instead, he instructed the rest of the team to enjoy themselves, with a reminder to rendezvous at the safehouse in three days' time. Sending them off with a hearty "Job well done!" I watched as my comrades eagerly headed out into the city, ready to immerse themselves in the excitement and energy of Dubai. As they disappeared into the vibrant streets, as their leader, I couldn't help but feel a sense of pride in my team, knowing that they would represent their organization with professionalism and dedication, even as they indulged in some well-deserved relaxation and revelry. Let's all believe that!

After their wild three-day leave in Dubai, the team gathered back at the safe-house, surprisingly, on time and all accounted for. It seemed that the allure of the bustling city and its various attractions had not led to any major mishaps or missing team members - a relieving outcome for Mark. Amidst the debriefing session, one team member sheepishly admitted to an unexpected incident that had occurred during their free time. It turned out that while indulging in the adrenaline rush of sand surfing in the desert, this team member had fallen victim to a stray dog's bite. I asked what was her name, jokingly, and he said, "Veronica," laughing.... Mark couldn't help but chuckle at the absurdity of the situation, deciding not to delve too deeply into the details surrounding the dog's unexpected involvement in their escapades. It was just one of those strange and amusing stories that often emerged from their line of work, adding a touch of unexpected humor to their experiences.

As the team settled back into the routine of waiting for their next assignment, fatigue from their whirlwind escapades caught up with them. After days of excitement and exploration in Dubai, they found themselves crashing and catching up on much-needed rest. Amid the quiet and somber atmosphere of the safehouse, the team members snoozed away, recharging their energy for whatever challenges lay ahead. Meanwhile, the team leader maintained his vigilance, patiently waiting for the call signaling their next mission. He couldn't help but savor the humor in the situation, finding amusement in the contrast between his team's exhaustion and his own readiness to leap into action at a moment's notice. It was all part of the unpredictable yet exhilarating life they led, filled with unexpected twists and turns, both in the field and during their rare moments of downtime.

As the team leader, I stepped outside the nondescript building to meet Mr. White, the enigmatic contact responsible for passing on our next mission. With a nod of acknowledgment, he handed me a folder containing the essential details of the assignment - the who, what, when, where, and why that would guide our next move. Upon returning to the safehouse, I attempted to make contact with the rest of the team, but no response came from the upper floors. Undeterred by the radio silence, I focused on the impending deadline - we had just 6 hours before "go time," and preparations needed to be set in motion swiftly.

Deciding to fuel up before diving into the mission details, I opted for a hearty meal to fortify myself for the challenges ahead. A satisfying plate of steak and potatoes provided the necessary sustenance to keep me sharp and ready for action as I mulled over the information contained within the mission folder. After finishing my meal, I ascended to the upper levels of the building to gather the team and initiate our strategic planning. The quiet anticipation filled the air as we convened, each member prepared to contribute their skills and expertise to ensure the success of the upcoming operation.

As we huddled together, the room buzzed with a sense of purpose and readiness. With the firm resolve to carry out the mission with precision and efficiency, we meticulously reviewed the details outlined in the folder, plotting our course of action and solidifying our teamwork to tackle the challenges that awaited us. Despite the absence of the elusive Serbian pilot, I remained unfazed, confident that he would be at the designated rendezvous point as planned, his engines purring in readiness. With a focused mindset and a sense of urgency, I quickly assessed the preparedness of the rest of the team, ensuring that everyone was in optimal condition and ready to embark on the mission at hand.

As the time to depart drew near, I issued a curt command, signaling to my colleagues that it was time to move out. "Pack your gear and leave nothing behind. "This is our moment" I proclaimed, instilling a sense of determination and efficiency in our movements. The two new team members swiftly cleared the room of any traces of our presence, ensuring that no valuable information or equipment was left unattended. Their disciplined actions exemplified the professionalism and attention to detail that was essential in our line of work. Stepping out into the cool night air, we made our way to the waiting truck where the rest of the team gathered, their expressions a mixture of focus and readiness. The sense of camaraderie and unspoken understanding among us spoke volumes, as we shared a silent acknowledgment of the challenges that lay ahead.

As we boarded the trucks, the engine's roared to life, the sound a prelude to the adrenaline-filled mission that awaited us. With a final glance exchanged between us, we set off into the shadowy streets, determined to face whatever obstacles came our way with unwavering resolve and a united front. Upon our return to the airport, a minor altercation had erupted between two police officers and the Serbian pilot regarding broken vodka bottles strewn haphazardly on the tarmac. An unforeseen expense of $200 was incurred due to this unexpected mishap, but such setbacks were merely a part of the unpredictable nature of our line of work. After the authorities were appeased and the situation resolved, we finally gained clearance to resume our journey. With a dismissive gesture, the Serbian pilot casually discarded another bottle, adding a touch of reckless bravado to our departure.

As we taxied down the runway towards the awaiting aircraft, the illuminated display of the international "Hello" sign served as a symbolic farewell to the chaos and drama that seemed to follow us wherever we went. Despite the tense moments and unexpected twists, there was a shared understanding among us that such challenges were an inherent part of the high-stakes world we operate in. In the background, the cacophony of multiple languages conveyed a sense of unity amidst the diversity of our team, each member bringing their unique skills and experiences to the table. The international "Hello" sign, with its message transcending linguistic boundaries, served as a reminder of the global connections and alliances we navigate daily.

As the aircraft gained altitude and the city lights blurred beneath us, we left behind the airport chaos and entered a realm where only our collective expertise and camaraderie would guide us through the trials that lay ahead. With a mix of anticipation and resolve, we pressed on towards our next destination, ready to face whatever challenges the mission would bring with unwavering determination. As we embarked on our mission in Asia, we found ourselves entangled in a complex web of intrigue and danger. The wealthy family member of a prominent leader had become the target of a radical terrorist group seeking to exploit their influence for nefarious purposes. Extortion was just the tip of the iceberg, as the true motives of the group remained shrouded in mystery.

Our task seemed straightforward on the surface - infiltrate the organization, identify the leader, and dismantle the faction from within. It appeared to be a bold yet achievable objective, sparking a sense of confidence and determination among our team. However, as we delved deeper into the operations of the terrorist group, we soon realized that the reality of the situation was far more treacherous than we had initially anticipated. The veil of secrecy surrounding the organization was impenetrable, with layers of deception and hidden agendas complicating our every move. Navigating the intricate network of contacts and covert meetings, we encountered obstacles and challenges at every turn. The delicate balance between maintaining our cover and gaining the trust of the group tested our skills and resilience to the limit.

In the midst of this high-stakes game of cat and mouse, we could feel the tension mounting as the shadow of the elusive leader loomed large over our mission. Unraveling the threads that connect the key players within the organization required finesse, strategy, and a willingness to brave the unknown. With each step closer to our target, the stakes grew higher, and the risks more pronounced. The line between friend and foe is blurred in the murky world of espionage and counterterrorism, leaving us to navigate a moral grey area where the boundaries of loyalty and duty became unclear.

As we braced ourselves for the final confrontation with the terrorist leader, we knew that the ultimate test of our skills and resolve lay ahead. The fate of the wealthy family member, the stability of the region, and our own safety hinged on the success of our mission. With a mixture of apprehension and determination, we prepared to confront the enemy within and fulfil our mandate to bring down the insidious faction threatening peace and security in the region.

CHAPTER 8

SAFE HOUSE

After arriving at the safe house, a sense of relief washed over us as we settled into the temporary sanctuary away from prying eyes and potential threats. The tranquility of the surroundings, with minimal traffic and a sense of remoteness, offered a stark contrast to the high-stakes mission we were embroiled in. The safe house, though modest, exuded a sense of comfort and security that was a welcome respite from the constant tension and uncertainty that accompanied our work. The brief respite allowed us to catch our breath, regather our thoughts, and plan our next move with a clear mind.

As we gathered around a makeshift table, our local contact shared crucial information that he had painstakingly gathered about a man linked to the terrorist group.

His dedication to monitoring the movements of this individual revealed valuable insights that could potentially unravel the intricate network of the faction. The local's allegiance to our cause, fueled by a combination of loyalty and financial incentives, underscored the delicate balance of trust and self interest that define our relationship. The exchange of payment, a tangible gesture of our commitment to his assistance, cemented our alliance and set the stage for a collaborative effort in confronting the common enemy.

The readiness of our local contact to risk his own safety and reputation for the greater good of dismantling the terrorist group mirrored the shared resolve of our team. The half payment provided upfront served as a testament to our mutual trust and willingness to invest in the success of the mission. United by a common goal and driven by a shared sense of purpose, we forged ahead with renewed determination and a deeper sense of camaraderie. The alliance between us and our local partner symbolized the fusion of different worlds and backgrounds in a collective pursuit of justice and peace.

As we prepared to embark on the next phase of our operation, the bond forged in the safe house served as a beacon of solidarity and resilience in the face of the looming challenge that awaited us. Together, we stood as a formidable force against the forces of terror, ready to confront the darkness with a united front and unwavering courage. The team had been on a demanding mission for months, navigating through rugged terrain and facing unforeseen challenges at every turn. As their leader, I understood the importance of not just strategic planning and operational efficiency but also the well-being and morale of your team members. With limited resources in the remote location, I took it upon myself to ensure that everyone was well-fed and nourished despite the circumstances.

As the sun began to set on another long day, I decided to prepare a special meal for the team. Knowing that they hadn't expressed hunger yet, I anticipated their needs and began cooking a feast that would replenish their energy and life their spirits. The aroma of hearty dishes filled the air, and soon the team members started to drift towards the makeshift dining area, drawn by the captivating scent and the promise of a satisfying meal.

One by one, they gathered around the table, expressing gratitude for your thoughtfulness and dedication to their well-being. Despite the exhaustion and challenges they faced, the simple act of sharing a meal together created a moment of connection and camaraderie among the team. As they enjoyed the food you had prepared with care and attention to detail, laughter and conversation filled the air, easing the tension and fostering a sense of unity and mutual support. My decision not to hire a local chef showcased my commitment to maintaining confidentiality and security within the team. In an environment where information was sensitive and trust was paramount, my willingness to take on the responsibility of cooking was always demonstrated a deep sense of security. By personally ensuring the quality and integrity of the meals, I not only provided nourishment but also reinforced the trust and cohesion among team members, strengthening the bonds of camaraderie and loyalty.

In the moments that followed the meal, as the team members sat around the campfire sharing stories and exchanging laughter, it became clear that my gesture had a profound impact beyond just satisfying their hunger. It symbolized your unwavering dedication to their well-being, my willingness to go the extra mile to support and care for them, and your understanding of the human elements that underpin successful teamwork in challenging environments.

As the night wore on and the stars sparkled overhead, a sense of gratitude and camaraderie permeated the team, forged through the simple yet powerful act of coming together over a shared meal. In that moment, surrounded by the rugged beauty of the mountain wilderness and the campfire, my team found strength in unity and resilience in solidarity, ready to face whatever challenges lay ahead, bolstered by the bonds of trust, and a few beers. As the team embarked on the reconnaissance mission in the unfamiliar village, every member took on a designated spot to observe and gather crucial information. The local guide led you to a quaint cafe tucked away in a quiet corner, where you blended in with the locals by sipping on steaming cups of coffee and casually conversing amongst yourselves. The cafe provided the perfect vantage point to survey the surrounding area discreetly while appearing to be nothing more than a group of travelers enjoying a break.

The clock struck 1500 hrs., the designated time for our "Target", to arrive. Tension mounted as the minutes ticked by, and each passing moment felt longer than the last. Finally, our target appeared. His arrival delayed by thirty minutes that seemed like an eternity in the context of your mission. Despite the delay, he quickly caught our attention with his furtive movements that hinted at a sense of urgency and caution. We watched intently as he entered a nearby store and emerged with a nondescript package in hand. Without a second glance, he swiftly mounted his scooter and zoomed off down the narrow village streets, leaving a trail of dust in his wake. The abbreviated route he took underscored the limited layout of the village, where everyone seemed to know everyone else's business and outsiders stood out like sore thumbs.

The waiting game had begun, prolonging the tension and uncertainty surrounding the mission. With limited information at your disposal and a sense of being exposed to the local populace, each passing moment heightened the stakes and emphasized the need for discretion and quick thinking. As the shadows lengthened and the day gave way to evening, the team huddled together, analyzing the feeting clues and piecing together the puzzle that gradually unfolded before them.

The atmosphere in the cafe shifted subtly, as the team members exchanged meaningful glances and gestures, communicating silently while maintaining a facade of casual conversation and observation. The challenges of operating in a tightly knit community where words traveled fast, and suspicions ran deep added an additional layer of complexity to the already delicate mission at hand. As the sun dipped below the horizon and the village settled into a quiet night, the team remained vigilant and focused, their senses tuned to the slightest disturbance or anomaly in the surroundings. The waiting continued, punctuated by occasional moments of tension and anticipation, as they braced themselves for whatever might unfold in the mysterious web of intrigue and secrecy that surrounded them.

In the midst of uncertainty and danger, the team relied on their training, instincts, and camaraderie to navigate the treacherous waters of espionage and subterfuge. Each member played their part in the intricate dance of reconnaissance, united by a common purpose and driven by a shared determination to see the mission through to its conclusion, no matter the obstacles or the odds stacked against them.

CHAPTER 9

IT'S NOT LIKE THE MOVIES

The following day dawned, bringing with it a sense of anticipation and focus as the team embarked on another day of surveillance and reconnaissance. Contrary to popular belief that their operations consisted solely of high-speed, action-packed missions, a significant part of their work involved meticulous planning, information gathering, and strategic revision to ensure precision and success. Settling into their positions, the team discreetly observed their surroundings from a new vantage point, blending in with the rhythm of daily life in the area. The familiar routine of sitting and waiting was punctuated by sips of hot coffee, providing a source of warmth and comfort amidst the uncertainty that accompanied their clandestine activities.

As the hours passed, a sense of patience and diligence prevailed, as team members engaged in subtle gestures and encrypted communications to convey crucial information and exchange insights without arousing suspicion. The facade of nonchalance and normalcy they maintained masked the intricate web of intelligence gathering and strategizing that unfolded beneath the surface. Contrary to the portrayals of espionage in popular culture, the true essence of their work lies in the meticulous attention to detail,the methodical collection of data, and the thoughtful calibration of strategies to adapt to evolving circumstances. Each moment spent in seemingly mundane activities held the potential for breakthroughs and revelations that could alter the course of their mission.

The process of gathering information, analyzing intelligence, and refining their plans unfolded gradually, akin to the careful crafting of a masterpiece where every stroke of the brush and every detail mattered. The team engaged in discussions, simulations, and rehearsals to finetune their tactics, ensuring that every contingency was accounted for, and every scenario was meticulously planned for.

Despite the perception of constant action and excitement, the reality of their work involved long stretches of waiting, observation, and precision planning. However, it was within these quiet moments of refection and preparation that the true mettle of the team shone through, demonstrating their dedication, skill, and resourcefulness in the face of challenges and adversities. Through persistence, collaboration, and a commitment to excellence in their craft, the team transformed seemingly mundane activities into vital components of their mission, laying the groundwork for success through careful preparation and strategic foresight. Day by day, they honed their skills, refined their approach, and worked tirelessly towards the perfection of their operation, knowing that patience and precision were key to achieving their objectives in the world of covert operations.

As we lingered in the cozy ambiance of the cafe, our focus shifted to the target we had identified - a young individual in his early twenties who held key information related to potential terrorist activities. Our mission required us to maintain careful surveillance on this individual, commonly referred to as our "mark" to gather valuable intelligence and insight into his activities and affiliations. The tense atmosphere in the cafe was palpable as we observed the young man making a brief stop at the store nearby. Seizing the opportunity, our local asset deftly tagged the scooter belonging to our target, a subtle but significant action that would allow us to track his movements and gather critical data without alerting suspicion.

With the crucial step completed, we settled back into our surveillance routine, knowing that patience and persistence were key virtues in the world of covert operations. Over the ensuing week, we maintained a discreet watch over our target, meticulously documenting his interactions, routines, and any potential leads that could shed light on the larger network he was a part of. The passage of time seemed to slow down as we remained steadfast in our vigil, blending into the background of daily life in the bustling city. Each passing moment was an opportunity to glean valuable insights and piece together the puzzle of the young man's role in the intricate web of clandestine activities that threatened the peace and security of the region.

Our days were spent in a delicate balance of surveillance and analysis, with hours turning into days as we maintained our watchful presence, ready to act at a moment's notice. The routine of sitting and waiting became second nature to us, as we understood that the painstaking process of gathering information and building a comprehensive picture of the situation required time, dedication, and unwavering focus. As the sun rose and set each day, we remained steadfast in our surveillance efforts, knowing that the information we were gathering could mean the difference between success and failure in our mission.

The synergy between our team members, the coordination of our actions, and the meticulous attention to detail all converged towards a singular goal - to neutralize the threat posed by the young terrorist and dismantle the network he was part of. Through our patient and methodical approach, we transformed the seemingly mundane act of sitting and waiting into a strategic advantage, harnessing every moment to uncover hidden truths and anticipate the next move in the complex game of intelligence and counterterrorism. In the midst of uncertainty and risk, our resolve remained unshakable as we waited for the opportune moment to act and bring our mission to a successful conclusion.

The frustratingly limited movements of our "mark" posed a significant challenge to our surveillance efforts, as he seemed to adhere to a predictable routine of visiting a handful of locations in a seemingly random sequence. The monotonous cycle of traveling from his house to the store, then to a rice paddy, followed by an orange grove and finally to his deceased uncle's house, which was now under the care of his aunt, offered little in terms of actionable intelligence. Despite our initial assumptions based on the sparse movements of the target, we continued to monitor his activities closely, determined to uncover any hidden patterns or deviations that could provide us with a clearer understanding of his motives and connections within the terrorist network. The stagnant nature of the surveillance operation left us doubting the reliability of the information provided by our local asset, fueling speculation about potential inaccuracies in the intel we had been relying on.

However, just when it seemed like we were stuck in a cycle of uneventful observations, a glimmer of hope emerged as the young man defied his usual routine and embarked on a daring journey, driving his scooter a considerable distance of 20 miles away from his usual haunts. This unexpected move sparked newfound excitement within our team, signaling a potential breakthrough in our efforts to track and intercept the target's activities beyond the confines of his usual territory. The sudden shift in the target's behavior served as a reminder of the ever-evolving nature of intelligence operations, where quick thinking, adaptability, and keen observation skills were essential in staying one step ahead of the adversary.

As we redirected our focus towards monitoring the target's movements in this new and unfamiliar location, we embraced the uncertainty and unpredictability of the situation, fully aware that this could be the pivotal moment we had been waiting for to gain a deeper insight into the terrorist network's operations. The investigative process became infused with a renewed sense of urgency and anticipation, as we strategized on how best to leverage this breakthrough to gather valuable intelligence and potentially disrupt the nefarious plans of our elusive target. The long hours of observation and meticulous documentation suddenly felt more purposeful and charged with a renewed sense of mission as we prepared to unravel the mysteries that lay beyond the confines of the target's usual stomping grounds.

With the thrill of discovery and the promise of new leads on the horizon, we braced ourselves for the challenges and opportunities that awaited us in this uncharted territory, ready to adapt and respond to whatever surprises lay in store as we pursued our objective with unwavering determination and renewed hope. The anticipation of the next day weighed heavily on our team as we meticulously planned our surveillance mission, relying on our local contact to secure a truck that would transport us to a safe vantage point near the mysterious farm. Despite the seemingly innocuous description provided by our local assistant, who nonchalantly mentioned that there was nothing of interest out there but a farm. We approached the situation with caution and a keen sense of vigilance.

As the designated pickup truck arrived to transport us to the designated drop-off point, we braced ourselves for what lay ahead, mentally preparing for the reconnaissance operation that awaited us. With a combination of nerves and excitement building within the team, we set out on the journey towards the isolated farm, surrounded by the vast expanse of wilderness and looming trees, shrouded in the veil of secrecy that masked the true nature of the location. Upon reaching our designated drop-off point, we disembarked from the truck and swiftly moved into the dense undergrowth of the bush, our senses on high alert as we navigated our way towards the farm. The silence of the surroundings was deafening, broken only by the occasional rustle of leaves and the distant calls of unseen wildlife, adding an eerie ambiance to our covert mission.

As we cautiously approached the farm, the stark contrast between the tranquility of the rural landscape and the palpable tension of our surveillance operation heightened our senses, sharpening our focus on the task at hand. Concealed within the bush, we conducted a thorough reconnaissance of the farm, carefully scanning every detail for any signs of unusual activity that could offer valuable insight into the target's whereabouts or intentions. The meticulous nature of our survey revealed subtle clues and anomalies that hinted at a deeper level of complexity beneath the seemingly ordinary facade of the farm. Each moment spent in observation and analysis brought us closer to unraveling the enigma shrouding this seemingly unassuming location, fueling our determination to uncover the truth and shed light on the hidden secrets that lay beneath the surface.

With each step taken through the bush and each piece of information gleaned from our reconnaissance efforts, we inched closer to unraveling the mystery that had brought us to this remote farm, ready to confront whatever challenges and revelations awaited us as we delved deeper into the heart of darkness that surrounded us. Armed with determination, skill, and perseverance, we pushed forward in our quest for knowledge and understanding, ready to decode the secrets hidden within the depths of the farm and emerge victorious in our pursuit of justice and truth.

As my team cautiously positioned themselves within the designated range, each member strategically placed to cover different angles around the target area, a palpable tension hung in the air. With no means of communication among us to maintain operational security, we relied on our training and instinct to coordinate our movements and responses, knowing that our success hinged on precision and teamwork.

Silently waiting and watching, we maintained our positions for hours on end, the passage of time marked only by the shifting of shadows and the gentle rustle of foliage in the breeze. As the sun crept across the sky, casting elongated shadows that played tricks on our perceptions, the anticipation of the unknown gnawed at our resolve, testing our patience and determination as we remained steadfast in our vigil. Just as a sense of resignation began to settle over us, a faint rumble in the distance heralded the arrival of the long-awaited trucks. A surge of adrenaline coursed through our veins as we focused our attention on the approaching convoy, our eyes locked on the convoy of eleven trucks that rumbled to a stop in front of the farm.

Our hearts beat in unison as we observed the unfolding scene before us, the tension thickens with each passing moment as the terrorists disembarked from the trucks with a purposeful stride. The atmosphere crackled with anticipation as the group gathered for their morning prayer, their voices blending in solemn unison, sending shivers down our spines as we remained hidden, observing their every move with keen interest. As the leader of the group stepped forward to deliver a commanding speech, his impassioned words reverberated through the air, drawing the attention of hiss followers who listened with rapt attention. The gravity of his message hung heavily over the scene, injecting a sense of urgency and purpose into the proceedings as the terrorists prepared to depart.

With a swift exchange of glances, my team silently communicated our next course of action, ready to spring into action at a moment's notice. As seven of the trucks rumbled to life and began to pull away, leaving behind a cloud of dust in their wake, we knew that our moment had arrived. It was time to execute our carefully laid plan and intercept the fleeing terrorists before they could disappear into the wilderness, their dark intentions reveiled in secrecy and treachery. As night descended like a comforting shroud over the surrounding landscape, cloaking our movements in darkness, my team and I prepared to execute our daring plan to apprehend the leader of the terrorist group. While the plan may not have been meticulously crafted or perfectly orchestrated, its simplicity and element of surprise breathed a sense of urgency and determination into our actions as we braced ourselves for the impending confrontation.

With a steely resolve and a quick assessment of the situation, I made the decision to strike when the leader least expected it, during his nightly ritual of taking a bath. Knowing that this vulnerable moment usually took place outback of the building, I formulated a plan to capitalize on this rare opportunity, banking on the element of surprise and swift action to secure our target before he could slip through our fingers.

Confident in my intuition and understanding of the leader's habits, I reasoned that he would likely let his guard down during this seemingly mundane routine, providing us with a window of opportunity to strike decisively and without warning. While the risk of detection loomed like a shadow over our operation, I trusted in our training and readiness to adapt to any unforeseen challenges that may arise along the way. As we stealthily crept towards the designated area, our senses were on high alert and our movements shrouded in the cover of darkness. I maintained a laser focus on the task at hand, my mind in a whirlwind of calculation and anticipation. With the rest of my team positioned strategically to provide backup and support, we synchronized our motions with practiced precision, inching closer to our target with each passing second.

As we closed in on the outback area of the building where the leader was believed to be, a surge of adrenaline coursed through my veins, heightening my senses and sharpening my focus on the task ahead. While no one may be directly watching the leader at that moment,

I was acutely aware of the potential risks and dangers that lurked nearby, ready to spring into action at the first sign of trouble. With bated breath and nerves of steel, I steeled myself for the pivotal moment that would determine the success or failure of our mission. As we were poised on the brink of confrontation, I reaffirmed my commitment to seeing the plan through, resolute in my determination to capture the elusive target and bring him to justice, no matter the cost.

CHAPTER 10

BAD PLAN

Despite my initial confidence in the plan to capture the terrorist leader during his vulnerable moment, reality soon reared its head in the form of unforeseen obstacles and challenges that put our mission at risk. As we moved closer to the outback area of the building under the cloak of darkness, it quickly became apparent that the situation was far more complex than I had anticipated. To my dismay, I discovered that the enemy forces were not only more numerous than expected but also fortified within an underground complex that presented a formidable barrier to our infiltration.

The realization that we were outnumbered and outgunned struck a chord of urgency within me, forcing me to reassess our strategy on the fly and adapt to the new circumstances with agility and quick thinking. Despite my penchant for slipping in undetected and swiftly incapacitating the targets - bag and tag, as I like to call it - the sheer scale of the enemy's defenses and the complexity of their underground stronghold posed a significant challenge to our conventional approach. It was a stark reminder that no matter how well-crafted a plan may seem, the battlefield is a dynamic and unpredictable environment where unforeseen speed bumps can derail even the best-laid strategies.

With adrenaline pumping and the gravity of the situation sinking in, I knew that our options were limited and our margin for error slim. The need for decisive action and adaptability became more pronounced than ever as we faced the daunting task of navigating through the labyrinthine passageways of the enemy's underground complex while evading detection and neutralizing threats along the way. As we regrouped and pivoted in response to the evolving situation, the weight of responsibility and the urgency of the mission weighed heavily on my shoulders. I knew that the success of our operation hinged on our ability to think on our feet, leverage our skills and resources effectively, and rise above the challenges that stand between us and our objective.

In the face of overwhelming odds and unexpected

obstacles, I resolved to stay true to the mission, to adapt and overcome with courage and resourcefulness, knowing that the true test of a leader lies not in the perfection of their plans but in their ability to navigate the tumultuous waters of uncertainty and emerge victorious against all odds. After conveying the disappointing outcome to Mr. White and facing the unexpected denial of the drone strike request, our mission took a swift and decisive turn as we were tasked with apprehending the target alive. With the sense of urgency mounting and the pressure to execute the capture mission intensifying, we swiftly regrouped and formulated a new plan of attack.

As we ventured back into the dense bush to track down the elusive target, the tension in the air was palpable, every step fraught with anticipation and the knowledge that the stakes were higher than ever: We were driven by a singular purpose to bring him to justice, by any means necessary. With adrenaline coursing through our veins, we pressed forward, guns blazing as we confronted the enemy forces head-on. The intensity of the firefight was only matched by the resolute determination of our team to fulfll our mission and secure the target. Amidst the chaos and the cacophony of gunfire, our overwatch team proved to be instrumental, swiftly neutralizing threats such as heavy machine guns that posed a significant danger to our operation.

In the heat of battle, a chilling moment unfolded as the terrorist leader was struck in the leg by a bullet, not from our side, but from his own people. The betrayal and brutality of war laid bare in that instant served as a stark reminder of the murky and treacherous nature of the conflict we were embroiled in. Undeterred by the chaos and the perilous circumstances, we pressed on with unwavering determination and coordinated precision. With each passing minute, the intensity of the engagement grew, every maneuver calculated and executed with precision to maintain the upper hand in the unforgiving battleground.

Finally, after a grueling firefight that tested our resolve and mettle, we emerged victorious, having successfully captured the terrorist leader against all odds. The sense of accomplishment and relief washed over us as we secured the objective and fulfilled our mission, knowing that our perseverance and teamwork had prevailed in the face of adversity. As we regrouped and made preparations to extract the target, the gravity of the situation sank in, underscoring the reality that in the unpredictable and volatile world of covert operations, success often hinges on the razor's edge of courage, strategy, and unwavering determination.

After successfully securing the target, we embarked on the challenging task of transporting him to a designated rally point, dragging him through the unforgiving terrain for what felt like an eternity. The strain of the arduous journey was palpable, each step a testament to our determination and resilience in the face of adversity. Upon reaching the rally point, our immediate focus shifted to tending to the target's wounded leg, applying makeshift first aid to stabilize his condition until proper medical attention could be provided. The sense of urgency and the need for swift action underscored the gravity of the situation, emphasizing the critical importance of ensuring the target's well-being while maintaining a secure perimeter to guard against any potential threats.

With the immediate crisis addressed, we reached out to our trusted local contact to arrange for transportation out of the volatile area. The uncertainty of the situation added a layer of tension as we awaited the arrival of our ride, acutely aware of the ever-present danger that lurked in the shadows of the chaotic landscape. Despite the apprehension lingering in the air, our local contact arrived without incident, navigating the treacherous terrain with skill and dexterity that belied the complexity of the operation. As we embarked on the journey back to safety, a collective sigh of relief swept through the team, tempered by the realization that the mission was far from over.

The bumpy ride back to civilization was filled with a mix of emotions - exhaustion. relief, and a gritty determination to see the mission through to its completion. The echoes of triumphant exclamations reverberated through the back of the truck, encapsulating the sense of achievement and camaraderie that defined our team in the face of adversity. As the skyline of the city loomed in the distance, a sense of accomplishment and relief washed over us, knowing that we had navigated through the perilous challenges and emerged stronger on the other side. The phrase "Dubai Baby" rang out amidst the shared sense of triumph, encapsulating the spirit of resilience and fortitude that had carried us through the harrowing ordeal.

In that moment, as we reflected on the events that had transpired, a deep sense of camaraderie and mutual respect bound us together, forging a bond that transcended the rigors of the mission and united us in the shared experience of triumph against all odds. Upon our return to the safe house, a sense of urgency permeated the atmosphere as we swiftly transitioned from the tumultuous mission in the field to the final phase of our operation - the crucial drop-off. The arrival of the waiting men signaled the beginning of the end, a moment that required precision and efficiency to ensure the seamless completion of our task.

With practiced precision, the exchange was executed flawlessly, the transfer of goods and information conducted with meticulous care that characterized our team's approach to every aspect of the operation. The sense of finality hung in the air, propelling us forward with a quiet intensity as we focused on the task at hand, knowing that our success hinged on the flawless execution of this critical step. As the drop-off was completed without incident, a collective breath of relief swept through the team, a silent acknowledgement of a job well done. The men disappeared into the shadows as quickly as they had appeared, leaving no trace of their presence behind, their efficiency mirroring our own as we prepared to vanish into the night.

Guided by the steady hand of our reliable local contact, we made our way to the awaiting plane, the roar of the engines signaling our imminent departure. The sight of the Russian pilot, a stoic figure in the cockpit, instilled a sense of confidence and reassurance in our hearts a testament to the unwavering professionalism and reliability that defined our partnership with him. With a sense of familiarity and trust that had been forged through countless successful operations, we boarded the plane, each member of the team taking their place with practiced ease. The Serbian pilot wasted no time in guiding the aircraft down the runway, the powerful engines propelling us into the night sky with a sense of purpose and determination.

As we soared into the darkness, leaving the chaos of the mission behind us, a sense of deep satisfaction and accomplishment settled over the team. The night sky stretched out before us, a vast expanse of possibility and potential as we hurtled towards our next destination, united in our shared mission and the unshakable bond that held us together a testament to the resilience, skill, and unwavering loyalty that defined our team in the world of high-stakes operations.

CHAPTER 11

HOSTAGES

The whirlwind pace of our operations had us moving seamlessly from one mission to the next, with no time for respite or reflection. While our initial plans to return to Dubai had to be set aside, a new and urgent task awaited us in a different country, thrusting us into the heart of a high-stakes hostage negotiation. The gravity of the situation became apparent as we learned that the wife and daughter of a prominent industrial leader had been forcibly taken, their lives hanging in the balance as ransom demands were made.

The perpetrators sought not only a substantial sum of money but also the release of some individuals imprisoned since the turbulent times of the 1980s, adding a complex layer of historical significance to an already dangerous and delicate situation. The weight of responsibility bore down on us as we delved into the intricate web of negotiations, navigating the treacherous terrain of demands and counter-demands in a bid to secure the safe release of the hostages. Drawing on our collective expertise and experience, we mobilized every resource at our disposal, meticulously crafting a strategic plan to ensure the best possible outcome in a highly volatile and uncertain environment.

As we immersed ourselves in the tense and fraught negotiations, the stakes could not have been higher. Time seemed to blur as we worked tirelessly to broker a deal that would tip the scales in favor of the hostages' safe return, acutely aware of the lives hanging in the balance and the far-reaching consequences of every decision made in the shadowy realm of hostage diplomacy. Against a backdrop of escalating tension and mounting pressure, we remained steadfast in our commitment to the mission, driven by a potent mix of determination, expertise, and an unwavering sense of duty. The clock ticked ominously in the background as we teetered on the edge of uncertainty, the fate of the hostages and the delicate balance of power in the region hanging by a thread.

In the crucible of the negotiation room, where every word and gesture held the power to shape destinies, we grappled with the intricate dance of diplomacy and brinkmanship, acutely aware that the smallest misstep could have far-reaching and irreversible consequences. The weight of the industrial leader's anxious gaze bore down on us, a silent reminder of the stakes at play and the lives that hang in the balance. As the negotiation unfolded with painstaking precision and calculated urgency, we navigated a labyrinth of conflicting interests and shifting alliances, inching closer towards a resolution that would determine the hostages' fate and the fragile equilibrium of power in the region. Amidst the swirling chaos and high stakes maneuvering, we clung to a glimmer of hope, fueled by the unwavering belief that our expertise, determination, and unwavering resolve would see us through the darkest hour, paving the way for a safe and secure resolution to a crisis that threatened to shatter lives and reshape destinies.

After the tense negotiations for the hostage situation were underway, the urgent need for specific electronic equipment arose. As we regrouped to strategize and plan our next moves, it became clear that traditional channels would not suffice in acquiring the necessary items within the tight time frame. In such high-stakes operations, it was imperative to have access to resources quickly and discreetly. Drawing on a network of contacts forged through past missions, I knew just the right person to contact for acquiring the electronics needed. The shadowy world of the black market beckoned, offering a swift solution to our dilemma. Despite the financial constraints we faced at the time, the allure of competitive prices and discounts in the underground market proved to be a tempting prospect.

Exploring the bustling underworld of illicit trade, I navigated the intricate web of transactions with practiced ease, leveraging my familiarity with the clandestine trade to secure a competitive deal. In the realm of black-market shopping, the mantra of 'buy 12, get one free' echoed through the dimly lit corridors of trade, underscoring the allure of bulk discounts and exclusive offers that only the underground market could provide.

With electronic equipment in hand, our focus shifted to the crucial task of establishing communication with the kidnappers. This vital step would serve as the linchpin in the delicate dance of negotiation and diplomacy, setting the stage for crucial dialogue and potential breakthroughs in resolving the crisis at hand. As we fine-tuned our communication channels and protocols, the weight of anticipation hung heavy in the air, each moment pregnant with the promise of progress or peril. Simultaneously, meticulous preparations were made to ensure the smooth and efficient transfer of the ransom funds. Counting every penny with precision and care, we meticulously organized the financial resources at our disposal, knowing that every detail matters in the high-stakes arena of hostage negotiation.

Yet, amid the whirlwind of activity and planning, a lingering obstacle loomed large - the demand for the release of prisoners from the 1980s. As the negotiations unfolded and tensions simmered, the prospect of acceding to this demand remained a stark and unmovable line in the sand. Given the unresolved historical implications and ethical quandaries surrounding the release of long-incarcerated individuals, the release of prisoners stood as a non-negotiable point, a steadfast principle that could not be breached, no matter the cost.

As we navigated the intricate web of negotiations and high-stakes machinations, the divide between what could be done and what could not be compromised became starkly apparent. The fine line between opportunity and obligation, compromise and principle, painted a complex tapestry of challenges and choices that would shape the ultimate outcome of the crisis at hand. And in the heart of the storm, as the countdown to resolution ticked menacingly onward, we stood poised on the precipice of uncertainty, grappling with the weight of responsibility and the unyielding demands of duty in a world where every decision carries the weight of consequence.

With everything meticulously set up and preparations in place, we braced ourselves for the pivotal moment, knowing that the waiting game was an inevitable part of the high-stakes scenario unfolding before us. Patience was a virtue we had to embrace, despite its lack of glamour, understanding that every second of anticipation was a crucial component in the intricate dance of negotiations. As the clock struck 5:00 PM, signaling the awaited call, a flurry of thoughts raced through my mind. The timing of the communication struck a chord; it hinted at a disciplined individual, one possibly bound by commitments or obligations that defined their schedule. Could this be a subtle clue to the identity of the caller, a piece in the puzzle of their persona that remains shrouded in mystery?

Intuition whispered that there might be a connection, a hidden thread linking the caller to the family in some cryptic way. Experience had taught me that such entanglements were often present in the intricate web of negotiations, where personal ties and allegiances lurked beneath the surface, guiding actions and decisions in unforeseen ways. A glimmer of reassurance flickered in the back of my mind, dispelling the looming shadow of a terrorist threat. The nature of the company owned by the caller provided a beacon of certainty amidst the uncertainty, offering a glimpse into their world and motivations. The puzzle pieces began to align, painting a picture that hinted at a different kind of complexity, one rooted in personal connections and familial bonds rather than nefarious intentions.

Navigating the delicate balance between caution and trust, we prepared to engage with the caller, armed with a blend of intuition, experience, and strategic foresight. The unfolding drama held within it the potential for both peril and resolution, a high-stakes game where each move carried weight and consequence. In the midst of uncertainty and tension, we stood vigilant, ready to decipher the enigma before us and unravel the intricacies of the situation with unwavering resolve. The call marked a turning point in the negotiation process, a moment of truth where alliances would be tested, motivations laid bare, and the path forward forged through the crucible of communication and understanding.

CHAPTER 12

THE DROP

Navigations in high-stake situations often walk a tightrope between conflicting interests, demanding a delicate balance of empathy, strategy, and resilience. While the essence of negotiations lies in the art of compromise and concession, the backdrop of emotions, motivations, and personal stakes can transform every interaction into a minefield of tension and uncertainty.

The specter of angry individuals, driven by a singular focus on financial gain, often looms large in the realm of negotiations involvingkidnapping scenarios. Their demands are underscored by a sense of urgency and desperation, they form a formidable obstacle in the path toward a peaceful resolution. However, beneath the facade of aggression and demands lies a more nuanced reality - one where the safety and well-being of the kidnapped individuals hang precariously in the balance. In this particular case, a distinct sense of unease lingered in the air, fueled by the knowledge that a family member was entangled in the web of uncertainty and peril. The emotional stakes have soared to new heights, blurring the lines between professional detachment and personal involvement. The weight of responsibility rests heavy on the shoulders of those involved in the negotiation process. Each word and each action carries the potential to either bolster hope or plunge the situation into deeper chaos.

Amidst the chaos and tension, the identity of the family member remains shrouded in ambiguity, casting a veil of secrecy over the unfolding drama. The mystery added another layer of complexity to an already intricate scenario, heightening the sense of urgency and importance of every decision made in the negotiation process. The need to tread carefully, balancing the delicate dance between revealing information and safeguarding delicate relationships, became a paramount concern in navigating the intricate maze of emotions and intentions.

As the negotiation unfolded, the intricate tapestry of personal connections, conflicting interests, and hidden agendas began to unravel, revealing the tangled web of relationships that defined the dynamics at play. Every clue, every revelation, held the potential to turn the tide of negotiations, to offer a glimmer of hope in a sea of darkness. And amidst the tumultuous symphony of emotions and motivations, the true test of character lies in navigating the turbulent waters with grace, integrity, and unwavering resolve. The shift of dynamics in the negotiations, marked by the revelation of an outside-the-city drop location, injected a sense of unease and urgency into the already tense situation. The prospect of a remote, desolate location for the exchange amplified the risks and uncertainties involved, casting a shadow of apprehension over the impending operation.

The reluctance towards such secluded drop locations, where the absence of witnesses and potential help increased vulnerability and heightened dangers, was not unwarranted. The inherent isolation of such settings magnified the stakes of the negotiation, leaving little room for error or contingencies in case the situation spirals out of control. Despite efforts to renegotiate the terms and request a transfer of the exchange point back to the city for added security and oversight, the steadfast refusal from the other party rendered any attempts futile. As the clock ticked towards the designated time of 1 am, shrouded in the darkness that both concealed and amplified the risks of the mission, meticulous preparations were set into motion to mitigate the dangers and maximize the chances of a successful rescue. The strategic decision to procure a dirt bike, along with the imperative modification to silence its muffer for stealth, highlighted the adaptability and resourcefulness required in navigating the uncharted territories of negotiation scenarios.

The deployment of Overwatch on the modified dirt bike, trailing behind with a watchful eye and a readiness to intervene if needed, served as a crucial element of the operation. The synchronization of actions, the coordination of movements, and the shared understanding of the mission's objectives underscored the cohesive teamwork and strategic foresight is essential in high-pressure situations. As the exchange neared, the tension in the air was palpable, the anticipation of the unknown electrifying the senses. Each member of the team braced themselves for the critical moment. The approaching tail lights signaling proximity to the drop location initiated a cascade of coordinated responses, dispersing the team into a synchronized display of stealth and readiness.

In the convergence of darkness, danger, and determination, the success of the operation hinged on split-second decisions, unwavering resolve, and a shared commitment to securing the safety and freedom of the hostage. Amidst the challenges of the external drop location and the heightened risks it posed, the unity of purpose and the strength of resolve propelled the team forward, navigating the shadows of uncertainty towards a beacon of hope and liberation. The pressure intensified as I reached the designated drop-off point precisely on time, conscious of the volatile nature of the negotiations with the high-strung individual on the other end of the line. Every step was measured, every action calculated, guided by the overriding priority of ensuring the safety and well-being of the hostage. The weight of responsibility bore down heavily as I contemplated the consequences of any misstep or hesitation that could provoke further harm or escalation from the other party.

Exiting my car, I embarked on the solitary trek, a solitary journey shrouded in uncertainty and apprehension. The gravel crunching beneath my feet echoed the heartbeat of the operation, each step closer to the drop-off spot laden with anticipation and trepidation. A quarter mile stretched seemingly endless, a reminder of the distance separating apprehension from resolution, danger from salvation. Leaving the ransom money meticulously arranged inside the safety of the car, a silent offering of compliance and negotiation, I took up a vigilant post, eyes scanning the surroundings for any sign of movement or activity. The stillness of the night enveloped me, a poignant contrast to the turbulent emotions roiling within, as I waited with bated breath for the pivotal moment that would determine the course of the exchange.

The stillness persisted, broken only by the beating of my own heart and the distant sounds of the night; the silence was a canvas onto which uncertainty painted its shadows and whispered its uncertainties. Time seemed to stretch infinitely, each passing minute laden with the weight of expectation and the burden of responsibility. The absence of a phone call, the expected signal of compliance and confirmation, cast a shadow of doubt over the proceedings, a question mark hovering in the darkness. Forty-five minutes crawled by, each second a heavy heartbeat measuring the passage of time and the endurance of resolve. The waiting, the watching, the silent communion with the night hung heavy in the air, a test of patience and fortitude in the face of uncertainty. And then, in a heartbeat, the stillness shattered, giving way to movement, to resolution, to the stark reality of the exchange unfolding before my eyes.

Walking back to the car, a mix of relief and tension knotted in my chest, I beheld the scene that had materialized in my absence. The hostages, freed from their confines, stood as testaments to the success of the negotiation. Their liberation was a beacon of hope amid the shadows of fear and uncertainty. The absence of a call, a deviation from the expected script, had given way to a tangible outcome, a testament to the unpredictability and complexity inherent in the delicate dance of negotiations under duress. In the aftermath of the exchange, the echoes of the night's events lingered, a tapestry woven with threads of risk, resilience, and redemption. The journey from drop-off to resolution, marked by moments of doubt and moments of triumph, bore witness to the unwavering commitment and unwavering resolve required in navigating the turbulent waters of negotiation in the shadows.

The aftermath of the ordeal left physical and emotional marks on those involved, the wife bears a visible reminder of the violence inflicted upon her. Despite the bruises and scars, both she and her spouse found solace in the relief that the harrowing experience was finally behind them. The raw emotions of fear and uncertainty gave way to a sense of gratitude and closure as they navigated the aftermath of the traumatic event.

With the successful retrieval of the ransom money, a new chapter of the operation unfolded, revealing unexpected connections and layers of deceit. The mother's keen intuition, honed by years of experience and intuition, immediately pieced together the puzzle when she recognized the voice of her sister's son, an unsettling revelation that cast shadows of betrayal and deception over family ties. The unraveling of familial bonds in the midst of a crisis underscored the fragile boundaries between trust and treachery, loyalty and betrayal.

The meticulous surveillance conducted by Overwatch, with its un-Alinching precision and unwavering focus, yielded a crucial breakthrough as they tracked the perpetrator to a warehouse --a recurring choice in the schemes of criminals seeking refuge in the shadows and anonymity. The convergence of information and intelligence propelled the team into action, a seamless coordination of movements and strategies honed by experience and instinct. The decision to converge on Overwatch's position, a calculated risk in the high-stakes game of cat and mouse, underscored the strategic acumen and tactical prowess of the team. Every member plays a vital role in the orchestrated dance of infiltration and apprehension, their disparate skills and expertise merging seamlessly in a symphony of precision and coordination.

As the events unfolded, the enigmatic figure at the center of the operation emerged from the shadows, a sketchy character driven by ambition and greed, a hunger for power and wealth that blurred the lines between impulse and strategy. The nuances of his motivations remained elusive, shrouded in ambiguity and complexity, a puzzle that confounded even the most seasoned members of the team. Navigating the intricate landscape of emotions and intentions, the delicate balance between familial ties and professional obligations came to the forefront. The tone of voice, the subtle cues that delineate boundaries between relationships, serve as a compass guiding decisions and actions. In the midst of uncertainty and danger, the unspoken language of emotions became a guiding light, illuminating the path forward through the tangled web of loyalties and betrayals.

The scene was a mix of tension and relief as the entire company gathered to witness the culmination of their efforts. All eyes were fixed on the figure being led out in handcuffs, the clinking sound echoing in the solemn air. The expressions of onlookers ranged from shock to satisfaction, a shared moment of closure after a prolonged period of uncertainty and danger. The smooth execution of the operation was a testament to the team's dedication and expertise, each member playing their part with precision and commitment. As the target was taken away, the collective sigh of accomplishment reverberated through the room, a silent acknowledgment of a job well done. The sense of camaraderie and unity among the team only heightened by the successful outcome.

Mr. White's elation was palpable, his satisfaction a boon to the a team morale. The phrase "Dubai Baby" resonated through the space, colloquial expression that captured the spirit of triumph and celebration. The promise of a luxurious getaway, a reward for their hard work and dedication, loomed on the horizon like a beacon of hope and excitement. The energy in the room shifted from tension to jubilation, laughter and pats on the back exchanged among colleagues who had weathered the storm together. The sense of accomplishment and unity permeated the atmosphere, forging bonds that transcended individual roles and responsibilities. As they basked in the glow of their success, the team knew that they were not just a group of colleagues, but a collective force capable of overcoming any challenge that came their way.

The End

9 798889 383563 2